Home for the Holidays

&You Anthologies

Home for the Holidays

A Christmastime Anthology

Edited & Arranged by

Nicole Frail

And You Press
an imprint of Nicole Frail Books, LLC
www.andyoupress.com

Contents

On a snowy December night, Tallulah curls up beside her Gramma, who begins to share a cherished memory from her own childhood of a Christmas Eve long ago with four sisters, loving parents, a candlelit church, and a snowstorm that nearly kept them from home—and Santa.

Madigan's friends, especially Luke, are disappointed but understanding when she has to miss their annual Christmas gathering to pursue work opportunities in the city. When a holiday party leads to a major disappointment, however, Madigan flees for the comfort and joy of home and those who love her best.

Claire is not looking for family when she takes a DNA test, and she's certainly not ready to love them when she finds them. But as a visit over the holiday break unfolds, she begins to wonder: maybe family can be found in the most unexpected places, and maybe, just maybe, she's found what she's always wanted and never had.

Shoemaker Marty Winthrop's niece, Phoebe, has one Christmas wish: to meet him. In the hustle and bustle of planning his trip, Marty forgets to buy a gift for Phoebe and ends up procuring a "good luck" dwarf from a local businessman before his flight. Little does he know, the dwarf may actually have a little magic in it.

It's Christmas in 1980s suburban Ontario, and one young woman finds herself caught between two branches of a family who love each other fiercely but live their faiths very differently. Determined to be the good goddaughter and the dutiful daughter, she navigates a day filled with small tests of belief, quiet doubts, and the kind of worry that only families can stir up.

When Megan returns to her childhood home in Venice Beach after seven years away, she finds her estranged younger brother, Max, already there. Forced to pack up their late parents' house together, old tensions flare, but rediscovered shared memories and spilled secrets begin the healing process, and decorating the house for Christmas makes them realize that reconciliation—and a new beginning—might be possible.

Introduction

Nicole Frail, Editor & Publisher

In early November 2025, And You Press celebrated a major milestone: the one-year anniversary of our very first anthology, *As the Snow Drifts: A Cozy Winter Anthology.*

And now, you hold our eighth in your hands.

And our ninth is in progress.

One of the best things about these collections is the community they create. Every author is invited to a group chat where they can make true writer/bookish connections with one another. They can trade ideas, share advice, and celebrate together. Sort of like a family.

Which brings me right to *Home for the Holidays* and its family-centered stories that highlight the important and inspiring relationships between siblings, children and parents/grandparents, partners, and even found family—friends, strangers, colleagues, and neighbors—this time of year.

This collection has all the staples of your quintessential holiday celebration: the anticipation of reuniting with friends and family, awkward dinner conversations, mugs of hot chocolate and elaborate desserts, gift exchanges, and just a touch of family drama.

We hope these stories bring you a sense of belonging, connection, and acceptance, regardless of where you spend your holidays this year.

Gramma's Christmas Eve

Gramma's Christmas Eve

Amy Kelly

My bones were sponges to the cold of the night. My hands ached as I closed the tattered book I'd been reading with my sweet granddaughter, a buzzing little bumblebee scrubbed clean in a flannel night gown.

"Time for bed, Tallulah." I leaned down to rub noses with her and mussed her honey-brown curls. The rocking chair creaked with the shifting of my weight.

My house was full of yuletide merriment: the soft glow of the lights from the tree, the shortbread cookies, baked fresh today and browned on the edges, set beside the tall glass of cold milk on the fireplace mantel. Nothing made me happier than when my son and his family visited. Warmth, connection, the tenderness of these three in my living room, I wish I could bottle this feeling and sip from it daily for the rest of my life.

"But Gramma, I don't want to go to sleep yet. Can I have another story? Please, Mom and Dad, can I?"

I took a deep breath, inhaling the nutty scent of browned butter, ginger, and my lavender lotion.

How could I deny those sparkling eyes?

My son winked at Tallulah and put his arm around his wife. "Now that you're seven, practically a grown-up, I think you can stay up a little later? That is, if Gramma has another story to tell."

My heart was full of admiration for the young man he had become, and a pang of longing for that little boy who once sat on my lap to hear these same stories. Christmas, such a time. A fulcrum that balanced past and present. All the old memories flooded back: baking cinnamon buns; laying gifts under the trees while the children slept; putting out tiny ceramic figurines from the nativity scene, my two children fighting over who unwrapped and placed the donkey. The edges grew fuzzier every year. But then with each new grandchild, more memories were born. All the more precious, because now I was aware that time was finite.

"I suppose I could think of something." I put the book down beside me and patted my lap to invite her to snuggle close. "Let me see."

"What about a story about when you were little, Gramma?" Tallulah curled up against me and looked up, into my eyes, awaiting the beginning of my next story.

A montage of happy Christmases ran through my mind, and I knew just the one to tell.

The moon cast a blue light on my family as we walked along the snow-covered lane. The piles of white weighed down the cedar bows, pulling them like theater curtains, opening to the clearing. There the old church sat with glowing, candle-lit eyes, welcoming us out of the cold.

"It's so beautiful." Amy squeezed her red mittens around her dad's ski gloves. The warmth of the church and her father holding her hand made her feel even more excited for the evening to come. She loved going to this church with her mom, dad, and four little sisters. Tonight, Christmas Eve, they would all sing carols from their pew before walking home. She pulled her dad's arm and led them up to the very front. The ancient faces of the parishioners stretched their wrinkled mouths into broad smiles as the five girls passed by with their parents.

"We are so glad to see the Smith girls have made it," Ms. Ethel beamed before taking her seat at the organ.

Amy wondered if this was what the wise men felt like when they presented their gifts to the baby Jesus. Her head drew a little higher. "Here are my sisters," she said to herself in her most royal voice. She was so proud of them all.

"I hope we get to ring the bell." Sarah pulled down her hood, smoothed her brown hair, and brushed the snowflakes from skirt. "Come on, Steph." She pulled at the girl's elbow behind her.

Stephanie's fine hair was pulled back in two barrettes, but she still managed to pull a strand out and twirl it while sucking on her two fingers. Amy watched Stephanie's eyes search the church, taking in the brown tones of the paneled walls, the cedar boughs framing the entrance, and tinsel winking as it captured the candlelight from the sconces. Briefly Stephanie took her fingers out to whisper to Zoe, Amy's second-to-littlest sister. Zoe leaned in. Amy thought Zoe had a dreamy quality about her; her hair was the color of the sunshine on a summer day, and it seemed to match her personality.

"Steph says she can't wait until Santa comes," Zoe said as the family was seated. Amy saw her dad exchange a smile with her mom, who was holding her smallest sister, Emily. The tenderness of it made her tingle all the way to her toes. Christmas was magic.

The churchgoers told the story of baby Jesus in turns, and they sang "Silent Night" and "Away in a Manger" in between. The sisters stood and sang, lending all the molecules of their hearts to each and every note. The songs grew louder as the night grew dark, and flecks of snow began to fall outside.

Sarah elbowed Amy.

"I think they turned off their hearing aids." The two girls smiled together at the group of elders who had pressed into their ears and were now singing louder and further offkey. The girls found joy in sharing a secret, and they squeezed each other's hands before returning to the hymn book.

Finally, it was time to ring the bell. The minister gestured to the Smith girls, who all beamed. Each of them needed a little help to pull down the weight of the giant church bell above them. Amy took the hemp rope. It was rough on her fingers, and she burned with embarrassment over the watching crowd, then brimmed with joy as she pulled to ring the bell above.

Ding.

The rope pulled her back onto her feet, and she struggled to stay on the ground, her toes straining in her black Mary-Janes.

Finally, it was over.

The girls zipped up their coats and pulled on their mittens. They could almost taste the delicious food Mum would prepare before Dad read them "Twas the Night Before Christmas" and they tucked into bed.

"Hang on, baby Emily needs a change and a feed," Mum said.

The crowd poured out into the night, which had become blustery during the service.

Amy, Sarah, Stephanie, and Zoe collectively took a deep breath.

"Of course, Mum. We were just excited to get going and have our dinner before Santa comes."

Stephanie, fingers still in her mouth, pulled on Dad's sleeve. In a voice reserved for the wingbeat of angels, she took her fingers from her mouth and looked up at him: "What if he comes before we get home?"

Dad scooped her into his arms and peered out the window. "We have time."

The snowstorm was a dense swarm of white bees obscuring the landscape. Stephanie frowned and looked up at Dad, who gave her a smile constrained by concern.

It felt like Emily was having a Christmas feast, including cranberry sauce, Amy thought as she stroked the whirl of brown hair atop the pink head that nursed in her mom's cradled arms. The rhythmic sucking and swallowing were soothing and matched the warm feeling Amy had in her belly as she watched her little sister nurse. Her heart had never imagined a baby so perfect.

The minister came in from seeing out the last parishioner, brushing off thick snow from his shoulders.

"Getting pretty wild out there. You might want to head out while you still can. There's supposed to be a blizzard tonight."

"Thanks, Dirk." Mum was just bringing Emily to her shoulder to burp. "We'll head out now."

"Merry Christmas." He walked through the door at the front. Snow blew into the church as he exited. Mum and Dad exchanged worried looks.

"Is Dirk coming back with a lantern?" Mum asked.

The family bundled up and opened the church door, heavy against the wind, which roared at the family as they stepped down the wood stairs.

"Watch your step." Dad held each girl's hand as their boots sank in the snow.

Amy, Sarah, Stephanie, and Zoe huddled close to their parents as they strained to see through the blinding white.

A glow appeared. A tiny ball that seemed to grow.

Dad used his loud principal's voice over the wail of the wind: "Must be Dirk with the lantern."

The family followed the light down the lane onto the main road. All was white, and Amy briefly imagined hugging a polar bear close and seeing nothing but its fur. The wind struck with icy lashes as the family continued in the flaky vortex. But the glow of the lantern persisted as they found their way to the house, finally.

"That's strange," Mum said. "I thought I turned off the lights."

The lantern headed back in the direction of the church as the family saw their front door emerge from the white. The house was alive with joy. Red, blue, and green lights danced and illuminated the garlands in the living room. The scent of greasy sausage rolls and cinnamon buns filled the air.

Everyone looked to the others in confusion.

"This food wasn't baking when we left." Sarah pointed to the kitchen. The table was full of creamy dips and sour pickles, crackers and cheeses. The girls' eyes widened at the food in front of them.

"And look." Zoe picked up a parcel. "These weren't here either." She shook the box and listened to the contents.

"It says: From Santa," Sarah said.

Mum and Dad were as lost in amazement as everyone else.

"Who could it be?" Mum said.

"You guys. It was *Santa*," Stephanie said.

The family ate the wondrous feast. After scrubbing clean, they put on fresh flannel nightgowns and were tucked in with their favorite Christmas poem.

When the lights were out, Amy watched the snowflakes fall from her bedroom window. A hush fell over her body and the house while everyone settled in for the night. In the distance, she could hear the jingle of sleigh bells, and she wondered if Santa owned a lantern.

As she considered the miracle that was each of her sisters and the love in her home, she knew that magic was real, and at Christmas, anything was possible.

"I love that story, Gramma." Was all Tallulah could say as she nodded off. My son lifted his sleeping daughter, and the three of us walked her to the little pink bed in my guestroom. We each kissed her forehead. Her mother tucked the comforter in tightly around her, just as she liked it.

This was the kind of love, warmth, and safety I had always wanted for my sisters, for my own children, and now my grandchildren. This was the magic of Christmas, and it was everything.

About the Author

Amy Kelly is a former midwife, current therapist specializing in maternal mental health. Her short stories have appeared in *As the Snow Drifts*, *Recipes for Romance*, 805 lit+ art, Scribbled, Dear Human, emerge25 (forthcoming), and Belladonna's Garden (forthcoming). Her nonfiction has been published in The Yummy Mummy Club and her poetry in Tiger Leaping Review. Her short story "Another Fish in the Sea," with Nicole Frail Books, was a #1 New Release for its genre on Kindle. Amy's YA manuscript *Little Acts of Useless Rebellion* was second runner-up in the 2023 Leapfrog Global Fiction Prize. She attended The Yale Writer's Workshop 2021–2024, SFU Writers' Workshop, and was selected for the McLoughlin Gardens Artist in Residency Program 2024/2025. *Waxing Arcadia* has been longlisted for the 2025 Leapfrog Global Fiction Prize. When not writing or working, she is tending to animals on her hobby farm, enjoying her two wonderful neurodivergent teens, or making pottery. Amy's last great adventure was hiking Everest Base Camp at age forty, and she hopes publishing her books will be her next.

You can find Amy on Instagram at:
@amykellywrites

To learn more about Amy, visit her website at:
www.amykellyauthor.com

Comfort Zone and Joy

Comfort Zone and Joy

Katie Fitzgerald

Twelve months ago, just before she moved to the city to pursue her magazine-writing career, Madigan Doyle chose a word of the year: *reach*. As she drew the word in large bubble letters inside her brand-new planner and colored it meticulously with fine-lining pens, she dreamed about what the year ahead would look like. She would reach higher, submitting freelance pieces to her dream magazines, hoping to get picked up as a feature writer. She would reach out to others in her field, building a network of contacts to help her advance. And most importantly, she would reach beyond her small-town upbringing to embrace sophisticated urban living among other writers with similar education, interests, and ambition.

Now, holding the cream-colored card in hand, and rubbing her thumb over the Christmas tree embossed into the thick, expensive paper, she felt a sense of accomplishment. Here was her very first invitation to a major industry event, *Aspire Magazine*'s holiday party. Madigan had only sent in two freelance pieces, so to be thought of as a worthy guest was shocking. She had checked the envelope four times to make sure it was her name printed on the front, and she had finally hung it on the fridge in her apartment so she could regularly reassure herself it was in fact addressed to her.

The only downside was the video call she was about to make. She hated disappointing her friends, even if she knew they would be understanding.

Luke's image filled her smartphone display instantly, and his contagious smile brought a grin to her own face.

"Hey, stranger," he said. He leaned as though trying to see behind her. "It's not looking too festive over there. Don't you have your tree up yet?"

Honestly, hustling for work had left Madigan very little time or energy for things like holiday decorating, but she didn't think Luke needed to hear that. "Not yet."

"Well, I just got mine. Wait until you see it. Laurel and Cody both said it's too tall, but it's not quite touching the ceiling, so *I* don't think so. And Fiona agrees with me."

Madigan tried her best to ignore the lump in her throat. "That's actually why I called. Um, I'm not going to be able to make it home for Friendsmas."

Some friend groups did Friendsgiving, but theirs loved Christmas movies and grab bags, stockings and cookies, sledding and drinking cocoa, so they had decided a December celebration was more appropriate. It had started their senior year of high school and had continued during every college break. Five years post-college, no one had ever missed a single gathering.

"What? Why?" Luke looked stunned. Madigan felt the same way. She had never expected to be the first to break with tradition.

"I got invited to a work party," Madigan said, trying to sound upbeat. "It's the opportunity I've been hoping for all year."

"Wow." Luke nodded, taking in the information. "Well, that's a bummer. Good for you, of course, but Friendsmas without you? What if we changed the date?"

Friendsmas was such an established institution in their friend group that nothing about it had ever changed. Luke had convinced his parents to rent their house to him when they retired to Florida, largely so that they wouldn't have to relocate their holiday gathering from the place it all began. That he was even considering changing the date showed Madigan how much this meant to him.

But even so, she couldn't. "I'll want to follow up on all the contacts I make at the party, so I should probably stay in town." It felt wrong to say it, but she thought there might be cocktail hours and New Year's parties, and she wouldn't want to miss her chance to continue reaching for success. "My parents will probably come here on Christmas Day."

Luke let out a long sigh. "Well, Mads," he said. "I'll really—*we* will really miss you."

Madigan caught that tiny flub and felt her cheeks flush. She would miss Luke most of all, too, but there was no sense in entertaining the idea of their relationship. He was content with the simple things he'd grown up with. Madigan was sure she wanted more. As long as she was here, and he was there, they could only ever be best friends.

"I'm sorry," she said simply. "Will you tell everyone I'll mail their gifts?"

"Sure thing," Luke said. "And if you have some time, try to give us a call so we can see your face, okay?"

Madigan nodded, realizing that if she spoke, she might start to cry.

Shopping for Christmas stuff had lost some of its appeal. As Luke defensively drove his shopping cart through Target, looking around for all the traditional things he needed to host Friendsmas, he kept having to remind himself over and over again that Madigan wasn't coming. Even as he counted everything before heading to the checkout, he realized how many things he should really put back. He didn't need whipped cream because everyone besides Madigan took their cocoa with marshmallows. He also didn't need five pairs of ugly Christmas socks, because Madigan wouldn't be there to wear hers. Same with the mint-chocolate cookies that only she ate, and the chocolate Santas with nuts that she preferred over the plain ones.

In the end, he bought it all anyway.

"Do you think she's going to change her mind?" Laurel asked when she came over to help with some of the baking. "Personally, I don't know if we'll ever see her again." Cody and Fiona felt similarly.

When they met up to cross-country ski after the first snowfall, Fiona said, "It'll still be fun, just us."

And Cody said, "There's a new paralegal in my office. Kyleigh. I could invite her. Maybe you'll hit it off, you know?"

For his part, Luke couldn't imagine what this holiday season was going to be like now. He and Madigan had danced around their feelings all these years, but he had always believed they would find their way to each other. Friendsmas always heightened that hopeful feeling, to the point that he wondered each December whether now was the time to lay it all out there. He couldn't just replace that kind of connection with a paralegal named Kyleigh.

Finally, when the night of Friendsmas came, he decided to prepare everything as though Madigan would miraculously show up, and he just hid all the extra stuff in the pantry so Fiona, Cody, and Laurel wouldn't give him anymore pitying looks.

Before he started the first movie, *A Christmas Story*, he took a selfie with the TV screen and texted it to Madigan while everyone else was stacking their festive plates with snacks. For the first part of the movie, while Ralphie waxed poetic about his Red Ryder BB Gun, Luke watched his phone for replies, but by the time Flick's tongue was stuck to the metal pole, he'd given up. She really wasn't here, and she really wasn't coming.

The party venue was beautiful, but Madigan had to admit it wasn't very Christmasy. There was a tree of sorts, but it didn't have a hint of greenery anywhere on it, and the ornaments looked expensive and breakable, like they would be a nightmare to put away.

She did like her dress, which had a white fitted bodice and a knee-length burgundy skirt, and the handbag she'd splurged on was a nice, complementary shade of green. No one was really talking to her so far, but the assistant editor of *Aspire* she had worked with on her two pieces was making the rounds, and she was really hoping to have a chance to get to know him better.

This was another way in which she wanted to *reach* before the year was over. If she was going to live in this city and work in this field, it made sense to have a boyfriend to match her lifestyle. Gavin Bainbridge was a logical choice for many reasons, and the perfectly tailored tuxedo he wore tonight made him look more handsome than usual.

In the meantime, she politely accepted hors d'oeuvres she was too shy to admit she didn't recognize and kept a smile plastered on her face so anyone who passed by would think that she was friendly, approachable, and having a wonderful time.

Once, her phone vibrated inside her bag, but not seeing anyone else scrolling or even taking photos, she didn't think it was appropriate to check her messages.

Finally, after a lengthy conversation, Gavin Bainbridge shook hands with someone at the next table, then turned his attention to where Madigan was seated alone.

As he approached, she tried to warm up her smile a little so it would look genuine, and she offered her hand. "Thanks so much for the invitation," she said in a cheerful tone. "It's so nice to be here."

Instead of giving her the million-dollar smile he had been flashing at everyone he'd met so far tonight, Madigan was met with a perplexed expression. "It's Madigan Doyle, isn't it?" he said, but her thrill at his remembering her name was tempered by the cold tone with which he added, "You got an invitation for tonight?"

Immediately, Madigan worried that she was supposed to bring the invitation with her as a ticket or something. "Well, I left it at home," she said, laughing a bit as her nerves kicked in. "But yes, I got it. Thank you again."

"Um." Gavin stroked his chin. "Well, we ordinarily don't actually host the freelancers at the holiday party. There's just so many of you, you know." He seemed thoughtful, as though working out a puzzle in his mind.

In the meantime, Madigan began to sweat. Was she about to get kicked out of her first major professional event?

"I might have taken a picture of the invite," she offered, cringing inwardly at how utterly desperate that sounded.

Gavin held up a hand. "I'm sure you got one," he said. "And please, feel free to stay this time. Obviously, there's been a mistake, but that isn't your fault."

Gavin might have said more, but after Madigan heard "mistake," she stopped listening. The Cinderella story she'd been imagining—where she and Gavin stepped onto the floor to dance to instrumental Christmas music and found themselves beneath mistletoe, and he realized the lowly freelancer was a beautiful woman—went up in smoke. Immediately after it went the professional dream, where she left here tonight with phone calls to make, emails to send, ideas to ponder, and stories to write.

"Thank you," she said hoarsely, trying to keep her voice even. But she didn't have to try for long because Gavin stepped away. He motioned to one of his underlings, then started whispering to him and gesturing in her direction.

Madigan couldn't stand it another second. Slowly, she stood from the table, placing her handbag under her arm and smoothing her skirt before exiting into the cold night air. She sank down on the nearest bench and, ignoring the cold, began to cry.

The entire movie had gone by, and Madigan still hadn't texted Luke back.

"I know what you're doing," Laurel said. "And you need to let her go. She's happy there."

"Or trying to be anyway," Fiona said. "It won't help her if we keep making her feel guilty."

"There's always next year," Cody said. "But she's where she needs to be right now."

But Luke couldn't shake the feeling that someone who was truly happy in a new place and who loved Christmas as much as Madigan did wouldn't have such a barren apartment and talk so much about networking. Excusing himself to grab a drink, he ducked into the kitchen and typed out another text to Madigan.

We're all thinking of you.

Before he sent the message, he set the phone down, squirted some whipped cream onto one of those minty cookies, then held it in his hand, pretending to take a bite. He snapped a selfie and then hit send.

He held his breath, and then three dots undulated beneath his message.

Can we talk?

Luke felt another twinge of concern.

"Hey, guys," he said, staring at the screen as he ducked back into the living room. "Go ahead and start *The Grinch*. I just need to make a quick call."

The looks they exchanged with one another as they all sat on the couch snuggled under blankets, feet in ugly socks lined up on the coffee table, told Luke they knew who he was calling, but they were kind enough not to say anything.

Quickly putting on his coat, he stepped out into the frosty night air then opened the app and video-called Madigan.

The background was pretty dark, but he doubted very much she was at the party. What appeared to be a streetlamp illuminated her face just enough to show him that she looked like she had been crying.

"Mads, what is it?" he asked gently. "Did something happen?" He stepped into a streetlight himself so she could see his face more clearly. "Are you safe?"

Madigan sniffled. "I'm safe," she said. "Safe and stupid."

"Never," Luke said, shaking his head. "What happened?"

"It was a mistake," she said, gasping as a sob overtook her. "I wasn't actually invited to the party."

Luke was confused. She had shown him the invitation. She was so proud of it, she'd probably had it framed.

"I don't know what happened, but I shook hands with the assistant editor, and he frowned at me, and I felt so small, and then he said I could stay, but I obviously can't stay. I mean, how humiliating would that be?" Fresh tears began to flow, and Luke longed to take her in his arms and console her. "Everyone knows I don't belong here."

No, Luke thought. *You don't. You belong here.* But he couldn't tell her that. It wasn't his call. When she left after last Friendsmas, that had been the deal he'd made with himself. He wouldn't use his feelings to manipulate her into staying. Now, he had to refuse to use holiday nostalgia and one bad night as a means of getting her to come home.

"You're as good as any of those people," Luke said. "One misunderstanding doesn't change that. They liked your writing, that's the main thing. You'll submit more next year and start fresh—"

"I want to come home," Madigan said, cutting him off.

Again, Luke was torn between the thing he wanted most for Christmas and being the supportive friend Madigan deserved.

His inner turmoil was resolved in two seconds, however, when Madigan said, "Will you come get me?"

In that moment, Luke didn't think through a single logical argument. He didn't ask why she couldn't go home and get her own car and drive there. He didn't suggest trying to find a train or bus. He patted his coat pockets, ensured he had his car keys, and began jogging to his own car.

"Yup," he said simply. "On my way." And he started the two-hour drive into the city.

They switched to audio once Luke was in the car, and the sound of his voice was such a comfort, but after the first hour, Madigan realized she was getting cold, even pacing back and forth, and that her phone's battery level had dropped below twenty percent.

"Why don't you go home, pack a bag, and be ready for me when I get there? If we're quick, we might catch the second half of *It's a Wonderful Life*."

That possibility was enough to bring Madigan back to reality. She was going home for Friendsmas. Home, to Laurel, and Fiona, and Cody, and, most of all, to Luke.

Her apartment felt different when she walked inside. Looking at it critically for the first time in many months, she noted the sterility of the place. It had no decorations on the walls, no personality. She didn't even have a pet for company, or a comfy blanket for her couch. The Christmas cards she had received from her elder relatives sat unopened on the counter, and the Advent calendar her mom insisted on buying for her every year was still in its cellophane. The only thing with any color to it in the whole apartment was the word *reach* written in multicolored calligraphy and stuck to the fridge.

Reach for what? Misery? Loneliness? Humiliation? As she set her packed bag on the floor in the kitchen, she tore down the stupid sign and tossed it into the recycling bin.

When Luke arrived, she was already in the lobby, eager to put as much distance between herself and that dreary apartment as possible. He didn't even have a chance to park the car before she came running outside to flag him down.

When she opened the passenger door, Christmas came drifting out. The stereo blared Bing Crosby, and she found a candy cane on her seat.

"I grabbed that when I stopped for gas," Luke explained. He shook his head, wiggling little reindeer antlers perched atop his head. "These too." He offered a pair to Madigan. "Come on, suit up."

I could kiss you, she thought, startling herself as she realized she actually could. But later, maybe. Too much was going on in her head right now.

On the highway, they sang along to Christmas songs, laughing each time one of them messed up a lyric. Luke revealed a couple more gas-station surprises: candy bars wrapped in festive snowflake packaging, a wind-up Santa Claus that wouldn't stay upright on the incline of the dashboard, and a lapel pin featuring a dinosaur in a Santa hat that played "Jingle Bells" when she tapped its tail.

Finally, giddy with holiday cheer, but bone-tired from the whirlwind of this intense night, they pulled up in front of Luke's house.

"The lights look great," Madigan said as she gazed out the window at the house where, for practically ten years, they had celebrated Christmas together.

"Better now," Luke mumbled, and when he realized Madigan had heard, he gave her that bashful smile she loved so much.

Inside, all three of their friends had fallen asleep on the couch with George Bailey's life story still playing on the screen. Madigan entered the living room just in time to see George and Mary dancing right up to the edge of the gymnasium floor as it opened to reveal the pool below. They fell into the water, and Luke touched her shoulder.

"What do you want to eat?"

It was after midnight, but Madigan didn't care. Creeping into the kitchen quietly so as not to disturb the couch sleepers, she sat with Luke in the kitchen and had the usual: cocoa with whipped cream, mint-chocolate cookies, chocolate-dipped pretzels, cheese and crackers, and a helping of lasagna. She thought back to those hor d'oeuvres at the party hours ago and realized the ordinary foods she had just eaten tasted so much better than all those carefully crafted, beautifully designed appetizers. She thought it had been important to leave her comfort zone, but now she was realizing the true joy to be found in the things—and people—she had always known.

There wasn't room on the couch, so after they ate, Luke sat on the floor beside the Christmas tree, and Madigan slid down next to him.

"I'm sorry tonight wasn't what you wanted it to be."

Twelve hours ago, she thought she had known what she wanted this night to be. Now it felt like a gift it hadn't gone that way.

"It was, though," she said.

He turned to face her in the colored lights of the Christmas tree, and Madi-

gan properly took in every detail of him for the first time. That stubborn curl hung down in his eyes, and his scruffy five o'clock shadow dotted his jawline. His eyes reflected the lights and the glow of the TV, and Madigan understood that this was more than Friendsmas magic. This was more than friendship, period.

"What?" Luke said, clearly unnerved by her staring.

"Just . . ." Madigan began, but words were insufficient. "Come here." Then she placed a hand on his cheek and drew him in closer, her lips, probably still flavored like mint, meeting his marshmallow-flavored mouth. For the first time all year, she was reaching in the right direction, and he was right there, reaching for her in return.

The next morning, Luke awoke to the sound of a shrieking hugfest on the part of Fiona and Laurel, who had evidently discovered Madigan's presence and pounced on her. Realizing he'd slept on the floor under the tree, he stood up and stretched his back before moving to stand beside Madigan.

"We didn't get to do presents," Fiona said when the initial excitement wound down. "*Someone* went gallivanting off into the dark of night." She looked pointedly at Luke, but he couldn't quite bring himself to feel guilty.

"Luckily, we all know how he feels about you, Mads," chimed in Laurel. "It wasn't hard to guess where he went."

Madigan beamed at Laurel, and that smile nearly knocked Luke flat. Whatever presents he would unwrap today could not compare to this gift.

Then Cody asked the question Luke did not want to contemplate in the least. "When do you have to get back?"

Luke froze, afraid of the answer.

Madigan looked thoughtful for a moment, but then a smile broke over her face. Locking eyes with Luke, she seemed to be asking his approval of her plans as she said, "I actually don't think I'm going back."

"No?" Luke wanted to be sure he understood what she was saying before he allowed himself to react. Was she seriously going to stay?

"No," Madigan echoed, shaking her head. "I don't have to be in the city to be a real writer. I can do that anywhere." Her smile widened. "And I want to do it where you are."

Now Luke felt like Scrooge on Christmas morning, ready to take on a whole new life. He grinned from ear to ear and put an arm around Madigan, pulling her close to him.

"Oh, hey," Cody said suddenly. "What about a new word for next year?"

Madigan groaned. "I don't know, I think I'm done with that too."

But as Luke leaned over to kiss her temple, several words streamed through his mind that he hoped would characterize the new year. *Together*, he thought. *Love*. And, last of all, his favorite: *home* .

About the Author

Katie Fitzgerald has been a featured author in three short romance collections and has published more than thirty short stories. Her short romances appear online at Spark Flash Fiction and Micromance Magazine, as well as in various anthologies. She is a 2024 Sparkie Award recipient for Best Romantic Suspense and has been nominated for the Pushcart Prize and the Cupid Prize. A graduate of Vassar College and a trained librarian, Katie resides in Maryland with her husband and five kids.

You can find Katie on Instagram at:
@katiefitzstories

To learn more about Katie, visit her website at:
https://bio.site/katiefitzgerald

A
Place
Called
Family

A Place Called Family

Caroline Baccene

Scratch, scratch, scratch. Why did I choose such an itchy dress, and, more importantly, why did I decide to wear it on a six-hour flight from Florida to South Dakota? Pulling at the awful fabric and almost dropping my carry-on, I continue making my way through the airport toward the check-in gate.

"It doesn't make sense to me. Traveling all that way to see some people you've never met." Daniel walks next to me, ignoring or oblivious to the stuffed bag slung over my shoulder, as he continues, "And you're giving up your break. Isn't that the point of being a teacher? So you can have all that time off?"

It takes a lot of willpower, but I manage not to roll my eyes at my boyfriend, and I'm wondering if it would be really rude to break up with someone during the holidays, especially when they're your ride to the airport. No, I need to at least wait until after Christmas. After all, I spent all that money on new headphones for him. Then there's New Year's, which is almost as bad as Valentine's Day if you're single. Just a couple more weeks and I'll cut ties.

"And why can't they come here? They don't want to meet their sister?"

Breathing a sigh of relief as I see the check-in desk has just a short line, I hoist my bag higher on my shoulder as I reply, "They have families. I've got the time, and if I don't go now, I'll have to wait until summer break."

He shrugs. "So wait until summer break."

Daniel just doesn't get me, which is nothing new. I've always felt like I didn't belong. Not with him, not with my family, not with anyone around here. And it didn't make sense until I got the results back from a DNA testing site and all these relatives I've never met started popping up. Of course, the first one I messaged was the man that had *Father, Shared DNA 50%* next to his name.

When I didn't get a reply for three weeks, I took the hint, logged off, and stayed off for a month. But eventually, curiosity got the better of me and I logged back in. And there it was: a message from someone that had *Half-Brother, Shared DNA 25%* next to his name.

Coming back to the present, I say, "Daniel, you don't get it. My biological father is dead. If I wait, what if someone else dies, and I never get to meet them? It's better if I go now anyway. The stress isn't good for me. All this wondering."

"What's there to wonder about? Your bio dad was a sperm donor. Your family lied to you your entire life. I don't get why you're going to meet this guy's *real* kids anyway. If I were you, I'd be going to my mom and demanding answers."

There's no way I'm discussing my complex relationship with my mother in the middle of an airport with a man I've only been dating a few months and probably won't be with a few weeks from now.

"Thanks for the ride. I'll see you in a few days." Turning, I give him a quick hug, which he returns, before I head toward the desk. Glancing back once, I see Daniel already walking away with his eyes glued to his phone.

I scratch the neckline of my dress again as I board a flight that will no doubt change the rest of my life. Or at least give me a great story to tell my future children one day.

My hands tighten on the armrests of my chair as the plane descends, having finally reached our destination, and I'm really grateful there's a former missionary sitting next to me. Surely God wouldn't crash our plane with her in it, especially when we are this close to landing.

"Well, I hope everything works out with your family, dear."

I don't bother to correct her, since I'm not sure she was even listening to me talk earlier. But if I did correct her, I'd be explaining these people are not my family. I didn't even know they existed until a few months ago, and you can't call strangers family anyway. Instead, I just nod my thanks and grip the armrests with all my strength as we bump onto the runway.

Once I've exited the plane, I stride past baggage claim, happy my lying mother at least taught me enough about airports to know if you don't have to check it, don't. As I make my way through the terminal, my eyes land on someone familiar, even though I know I've never met him before. When he meets my eyes, I stumble a bit before smoothing my pace and approaching. It's like I'm looking in a masculine mirror: dark red hair that's more straight than curly, caramel eyes, a nose that's just a bit too large for its face. If it weren't so freaky, I'd laugh at the similarities.

Next to the man is a beautiful woman that doesn't look a thing like him. Dark hair, olive skin, and much shapelier than either of us. Yet she's the one who jumps up and down, squealing as she says something to my male twin. They meet me in the middle, where she throws her arms around me and squeezes. The man stays a step behind as he sighs and shrugs an apology at me.

"If you aren't Claire, I'm a Pisces!" The exuberant female releases me and backs up, smiling bright white teeth at me. "I'm Dana. This is my brother, Samuel. Or I guess, *our* brother. Gosh, is that weird or what? This is *our* brother, Samuel."

Samuel shakes my hand and says, "You'll have to excuse Dana. She's the most annoying person you'll ever meet."

Dana rolls her eyes and takes a step back. "Come on. We're parked in the closest garage. Let's go!" Then she turns and heads toward the exit, bouncing more than walking.

"She's really excited you're here." Samuel grabs the bag off my shoulder and hoists it on his before continuing. "I know what you're thinking, and no, it's not going to be that terrible."

He starts walking after Dana, and since they are my ride and now have my luggage, I take a deep breath and fall into step next to him, really hoping this trip wasn't a huge mistake.

I learn a few things in the next forty-five minutes as we make our way to where I'll be staying for the next few days. One: South Dakota is freezing in December. Obviously, I knew it'd be nothing like Florida, but I didn't realize just how different other parts of the United States are. Samuel quietly shrugged off his coat and handed it to me when he saw I was severely underdressed. Normally, I'd never take a stranger's jacket, but like I said, it is *freezing* here.

Two: I shouldn't have worried about it being awkward or having to think of stuff to say. Dana never stops talking. I'm pretty sure she chugged five espressos waiting for me at the airport. What's good about this is I don't have to worry about the flow of the conversation, and she's like an open book. Samuel is not like this, which brings me to number three: He's much quieter than Dana. Therefore, it's hard for me to get a read on him. I have no idea if he's happy to meet me or upset his father was a sperm donor. Honestly, I have no idea what he's thinking. Although I suppose they might say the same about me.

But he must've been curious enough about the situation to invite me to visit. Or had I invited myself? It's possible I mentioned coming to visit, but he was the one who suggested I stay with them, which was probably a bad idea. Who goes to another state and stays with complete strangers for multiple days? Someone who makes a teacher's salary and can barely afford the flight, that's who.

"But college is okay. I can't complain. We're here!"

Dana opens her door before Samuel has come to a complete stop, and I look around before exiting the warm vehicle. A large farmhouse sits in the middle of a tidy yard. Tidy from what I can see, which isn't much from all the snow. There's a field on one side and what looks like a forest on the other. Besides a detached garage, a couple of storage sheds around the property, and what might be a barn, there's not another building in sight.

This was definitely a mistake.

What if these people are insane?

What if I'm about to get murdered and made into stew or something?

Before I can figure out what to do, my door opens, blasting cold wind on my face.

"Come on, Claire! It'll only get colder when the sun sets!"

Deciding any other death is preferable to freezing out here, I climb out of the backseat and follow them into the house.

Delicious warmth fills me as soon as I enter the front door. I say delicious because the smell of baked goods hits me at the same time the heat does, making me sure that if I'm going to die, I'd rather do it in here than out there.

"Mom, this is Claire, one of Dad's *other* children."

My eyes take a moment to adjust from the bright white reflection of the snow to the dimly lit entryway, but when they do, a short, round, middle-aged woman who looks similar to Dana is approaching with a much kinder smile than I was expecting.

"Claire, how wonderful to meet you, darling. My name is Wanda." Dana's mom looks me up and down before pulling me into an embrace. What is it with this family and all the touching? "Oh my goodness, dear. You look exactly like your father."

Not bothering to correct her and tell her that *my* father was a drug addict that abandoned my family when I was a child and died a few years later, I just give my typical subdued smile and pat her cautiously on the back before taking a step back. The woman has freaking tears in her eyes, and now I am positive this trip was a mistake. I'm here to meet the people that share my blood, not take this lady down memory lane or comfort a sad widow.

"Come on. I'll show you the guest room."

Grateful for Samuel's excuse to extract myself from this woman's arms, I follow him up a large wooden staircase wrapped with Christmas garland and into a pretty room with what looks like antique furniture. In fact, the entire house looks like it's from the year 1900.

"So, once you're settled in, we were talking about showing you around town. It's small but has a few cool shops and restaurants."

Internally sighing at the prospect of staying here for multiple days, I just smile and reply, "Sounds good."

Nodding, he turns to leave before he stops. "We may have different ways of showing it, but we are all really glad you're here, Claire. I can't imagine it's easy for you, but thanks for being brave enough to come out here."

Stopping him before he can leave the room, I ask, "What about you? This isn't . . . weird for you guys?"

Samuel leans his shoulder against the doorframe and sighs, thinking for a moment before replying. "Whether you knew it or not, you've always been in our lives. We knew you existed out there somewhere for as long as I can remember. It wasn't a secret that he was a sperm donor. Dad talked about being poor before he met my mom. But there are a lot of ways for a young guy to make money without having to sell his sperm, so I think he liked the idea of having other kids out there. Before he got sick, he'd talk about one day wanting to have a huge family reunion with all his kids."

"He has other kids?"

"You're the first we've met, but surely there are more out there. He was a monthly sperm donor for over two years. Then he met my mom, got married really fast, and they got pregnant with me even faster."

Over two years? Twelve donations a year. And do they just get one kid from each donation or can they get more? We're talking about the possibility of twenty-four kids. Could be fewer but could also be more for all I know. Although if they were out there, why wouldn't they do DNA testing to find him? Maybe they did. Maybe they used a different testing site than Samuel and I did. Or maybe they don't know they were donor babies. I mean, I didn't. How many siblings do I have out there that have no idea the dad they grew up with isn't their biological dad?

Samuel breaks me out of my whirlwind of thoughts by sitting next to me on the bed where I must have ended up when he dropped that bombshell on me. I'm grateful he isn't as touchy-feely as his mom and sister. He doesn't even sit very close. It's nice. Like I'm not alone, but I'm not being smothered.

"There's no pretending I know what you're going through, just like you can't know how we feel about it. But trust me, we are all really happy to meet you."

There's a tightness in my throat that doesn't go away when I clear it, but I try to ignore it as I reply. "I just wanted to find out more about my mom's lineage.

Thought it'd be cool to see where our family was from. Then one day I logged in, and your dad popped up." I snort. "I thought my mom had an affair on my dad."

Playing with a loose strand on the hem of my dress, I continue. "I confronted my mom when his name came up as my father on the site. We don't have a good relationship, but I thought she'd at least tell me the truth." A humorless laugh escapes me. "She denied the affair, which I thought was a lie. But she didn't even tell me about going to a sperm donor. In fact, she insisted the man who lived with us until I was six years old was my biological father. It doesn't make any sense, and she refuses to even talk to me about it. Why was she even in South Dakota anyway?"

Since my question is clearly not meant for him, Samuel doesn't bother replying, and we just sit in silence for a while. But it's one of the nicest silences I've ever experienced.

Two days pass, which is both a positive and a negative. Negative because there's only one more day before I return to Florida, and despite everything, spending a couple of days with a nice family isn't a bad way to spend a portion of my Christmas break. And this family does all the Christmas stuff; ice skating, walking through Christmas lights, buying hot cocoa, shopping for presents. It's like I've been thrown into a Hallmark movie.

Positive because I don't know how much more I can listen to the deceased man that gave me half of *my* DNA be referred to as my dad. Dana is the worst offender, although that could be because she talks so much. The girl seriously doesn't stop when she gets started, and it seems like she's decided to tell me every fact about her father she knows.

"But that's the thing about Dad. He was always a thoughtful guy, more of a thinker than a talker." We are sitting on the porch swing, bundled up in all manner of clothing and blankets to fight off the cold temperatures, but I have to admit, the view is pretty spectacular, and the hot tea helps with the chill too. "More like Samuel in that way. And you."

I take a deep drink from my mug and try to ignore the comment that I am anything like her dad, but I've already had to sit here and listen to her talk about how I look like him, act like him, and even walk like him.

Dana continues. "But I mean, that's to be expected, I guess. I just wish I'd gotten that trait from him, too. Two out of three of his kids got it though, so I guess it's good our dad passed that on to sixty-seven percent of his children."

The sound of my mug hitting the table next to us is a little louder than I intended, but it doesn't stop me from standing and taking a step toward the front door to get away.

"What's wrong?"

I turn, ignoring Dana's confused and slightly hurt expression, and reply, "What's wrong? Dana, he's not *my* dad. He's a man who donated some DNA twenty-six years ago. I never met him. I didn't even know he existed until three months ago. You keep saying all these things about *my* dad. But *my* dad left me when I was a child. I have only a few memories of him, and they involve him being either strung out or passed out. That was my childhood. Your childhood was great. I get it. You had a wonderful dad. I'm happy for you. *But he wasn't my dad.* Samuel isn't *my* brother. You aren't *my* sister. You people are strangers, so quit acting like that's not the case."

My words hit her hard, and I instantly regret them. When I started talking, I didn't mean to say those things. They tumbled out of me before I could stop them. And I can see the damage they inflict, like a car crash moving in slow motion. I run inside before I can see the amount of wreckage I leave behind, almost knocking into Samuel, who was heading outside. Based on his expression, he must have heard everything, but I go upstairs to the guest room before I can analyze if I've hurt him, too.

Once I shut the door, almost instantaneously my bag is on the bed and I'm throwing my clothes into it. My hands become blurry, and it takes me a moment to realize there are tears in my eyes. Not bothering to wipe them away, I keep packing, just desperately wanting to leave and forget about these people.

There's a light tap on the door, and a huge part of me wants to just ignore it until they leave, but even though my childhood had some problems, I wasn't raised to be rude.

Expecting Dana to be on the other side in tears, I'm surprised to see Samuel there, leaning against the door, his expression not giving anything away. Opening the door a bit wider, he takes a step inside. Maybe this is the part where he screams at me for being awful to his sister. Maybe this is when he kicks me out into the cold to wait for a cab, throwing my belongings in the snow next to me.

I go back to stuffing my bag while he leans against the wall and quietly says, "I get it. My dad wasn't your dad. And I'm not your brother. Biologically, we share some DNA. But did we grow up pulling each other's hair or fighting over the last chocolate chip cookie? No. I was here. You were there. The only reason we are where we are now is because of some technology that didn't even exist a few years ago."

Zipping the last of my belongings into my bag, I turn to face him. I don't get the chance to agree or disagree with his words before he's continuing.

"But I could be. Your brother, I mean. And Dana could be your sister. My mom isn't your mom, but she's one hell of a listener and makes a great chocolate chip cookie." He takes a step out of the doorway but maintains eye contact. "You're not alone if you don't want to be. You're only not family if you don't want to be."

With those words, he turns and walks away, and as his footsteps echo down the hallway, I'm stuck wondering if maybe they could be my family. Like, not just on paper but really family. The kind that invites me down every Christmas and comes to my wedding one day. The kind that sends me stupid GIFs in the middle of the night for no other reason than it made them think of me. The kind I call when I go through a rough breakup or have a fight with my mother or have a question about how to fix the leak in my sink. Those people downstairs are more than just some names on a piece of paper saying we come from the same gene pool, aren't they?

With a deep breath, I leave my bag on the bed and slowly make my way back downstairs, expecting Dana to scream at me or her mother to grab me by the arm and shove me out into the snow. Instead, I find Samuel in the kitchen pouring a glass of milk while his mom plates *chocolate chip cookies* fresh out of the oven. I can see Dana in the living room watching television and know that's where I need to be. So, I quietly make my way to the couch and sit next to her. Neither of us says anything. Neither of us does anything as we stare at the old sitcom from the 1950s playing on the screen in front of us. I'm at a loss for words and terrified of what she'll say when she finally does open her mouth.

But after a few minutes, Dana just scoots over the foot separating us and rests her head on my shoulder. She doesn't say anything, just leans against me and continues watching. So I just stay there and let my sister lean against me. She doesn't realize she's the one holding me up.

"Here you go, girls. Get them before they're all gone." Wanda hands us each a plate with two cookies. Dana shoves one of hers into her mouth before I've even managed to pick up a cookie. But when I do take a bite, I understand the rush completely. Samuel was right. The best damn cookie I've ever eaten. Without even comprehending my motions, that one has disappeared into my mouth and the second one has a bite taken out of it. Although, just as I'm about to follow Dana's lead and stick the other half of my final cookie in my mouth, someone tugs my hair from behind.

When I turn to look, Samuel snatches the cookie out of my hand as he walks by, sticking it into his mouth and taking a seat next to me on the couch so I'm sandwiched between them. He sits back and rests his arm on the back of my cushion as he says, "Remember when Dad would make us stay up super late watching this show? All the time. Even on school nights."

Dana laughs as she returns to her position leaning against me. "Make us? I'm pretty sure we were very willing."

"If my memory is accurate, you guys would make *him* stay up all night." Wanda sits on the recliner next to us and sighs with what I can only assume is the smile of someone who loved and lost but would do it again in a heartbeat.

And I know in that moment, as the Christmas tree lights blink in the corner of my vision, the black-and-white television show playing in front of me, and my two siblings on either side of me, this is what family is. And I want it. For the rest of my life.

Five Years Later

"We're almost there! Quit freaking out. I just saw you a few months ago."

My voice as I exit the baggage area is a bit louder than I meant it to be, causing an old man next to me to give me a dirty look. I ignore him and roll my suitcase past him as I hoist the baby sling higher on my chest and almost drop my phone from the crook of my shoulder.

Dana's laugh comes from the other end. "Oh my gosh, I can hear you all the way across the airport. And I haven't seen you since summer! That was six months ago. Wait! I see you! Where's John?"

Glancing around me, I find Dana waving exuberantly and hopping up and down. Next to her is Samuel with his two boys, who all wave and smile as we make our way toward each other.

"He had to work, but he's flying out tomorrow."

"Couldn't wait one more day to see us, huh?"

"Honestly, that's the truth." At this point we've reached each other, so I hang up the phone.

"Aunt Claire Bear!" My three-year-old twin nephews grab me by the legs and squeeze.

"How are my favorite boys?"

Dana interrupts our reunion. "There's my beautiful niece! Oh my goodness. She's gorgeous!" Dana holds out her hands, so I gingerly take my half-awake daughter out of her carrier and pass her over. "Oh, Claire. She's lovely."

My daughter looks up at Dana with curious eyes but doesn't cry, which is a miracle in itself. Samuel reaches around and gives me a side hug. "Hey, there."

Surrounded by my family, I return his hug and grin.

About the Author

Caroline Baccene is the author of the novels *Breathing in the Fog* and *A Beautiful Lily*, as well as the short stories "The Charred Grape," "When You Know, You Know," "Of Sound Mind," "A Place Called Family," and "One Perfect Gift." Caroline grew up in the middle of nowhere, South Carolina, where she developed a love of reading, writing, acting, gardening, and caring for all types of animals. She graduated from the University of South Carolina with a degree in Early Childhood Education and was a teacher for five years. She currently resides in South Carolina with her husband and son.

You can find Caroline on Instagram at:
@caroline_baccene

To learn more about Caroline, visit her website at:
carolinebaccene.com

The Advent-ures of Phoebe's Christmas Dwarf

The Advent-ures of Phoebe's Christmas Dwarf

Nat Bickel

December 1982

This was the last driveway Marty would shovel. His flight to Illinois was tomorrow morning, and he had met almost every neighbor since he shifted his Christmas plans at the start of December. He would make it to his sister's house on December 24, Christmas Eve, and just in time to grant Phoebe's only wish.

The last bit of snow gathered on the blade of the shovel, his shoulders aching at the weight of the conglomerate of what he liked to think of as powdered sugar. His stomach growled from his daydream of endless donuts. Dumping the last heap to the side, he salted the end of the driveway to finish the job. As the setting sun glinted off the freshly plowed pavement, he suspected the same sparkle showed in his own eye. He collected his payment and began the cold walk home when panic struck him. He hadn't even purchased a gift for little Phoebe. Sure, his niece's only wish was to see him, but if he arrived empty-handed, it would come across as thoughtless, especially to his sister and her husband.

A block away from his home, he noticed a dim light still shone in the window of a local hardware shop that doubled as a woodworking business. Marty turned the doorknob, but it was locked. Calvin, the owner, walked out from the back of the store and peered through the window. Marty had mended many work boots for Calvin, and recognition immediately showed on his face. He unlocked the door, greeting Marty as he shivered from the cold.

"What can I help you with, Marty?" Calvin asked, looking past him at the empty, snow-covered streets. "Technically, we're closed, seeing tomorrow's Christmas Eve, and most people are at home with their families," Calvin said, distracted by Marty's dirt and slush-coated ski pants. "Say, what's a shoemaker doing out in the snow at this time of evening?"

"Just finishing up a side job clearing driveways. Trying to get to my niece for Christmas," Marty said, peeling off his gloves. "I know this is last minute, but is there anything in your shop a six-year-old would like?"

"Marty, you're asking a hardware store owner for a gift for a little girl?" Calvin replied, chuckling.

"It sounds awful, but I completely forgot about a gift. I've been so focused on getting to her that the thought never crossed my mind. I'm desperate. Maybe a gardening trinket?" In this head, Marty called up the small, high-pitched, faint voice he heard on the phone and felt a sense of urgency.

"We mostly have gardening tools . . ." Calvin trailed off as he put up a finger and walked toward the back of the store to the workshop. Calvin passed nails, wrenches, and paused at a bucket, surely trying to think of some sort of use a six-year-old would have for it, before he continued into the workshop. Marty waited while sounds of rummaging echoed.

"What about this?" Calvin asked, holding up what looked like a deranged elf.

"What is it?" Marty's could feel the look of displeasure as it came over his face.

"The other day, an elderly man dropped this off along with blueprints of a dog house for his first pup. He mentioned that he worked for a toy factory in town, and whenever a toy doesn't come out just right, it's good luck. This here is a good luck dwarf. If you look closely, one of his ears is bigger than the other. Instead of tossing him and others who turn out similarly, he gives them to people in hopes the luck will live on," Calvin finished.

Marty stared at the somewhat misshapen dwarf, noticing the ugly, yet eccentric nature of the toy. One ear did look much bigger than the other, but he thought maybe Phoebe would find him cute, something to add to the collection of toys he assumed she had. Maybe she wouldn't even play with him, but at least he wouldn't walk into Alex and Norvi's home empty-handed.

"I'll take him," Marty said as he placed the dwarf in his coat pocket, handing over a few bills with thanks to Calvin before heading back out into the night, ready to get some sleep before his early morning flight.

Marty buckled his seatbelt while the flight attendant motioned to the exit doors. He took note of the potential escape route, nerves creeping in. This was his first flight. The engines started to grow louder as the plane geared up for its ascent. Marty leaned his head back against the seat and closed his eyes while the plane grew in speed until it was finally safe enough for the pilot to pull back on the yoke and lift off. It reminded him of himself. He'd never gone fast a day in his life—always slowing things down and pulling back if they got too much momentum.

Marty Winthrop was a shoemaker by trade, or as the locals called him, a shoe healer. His father had taught him when he was only sixteen, and he'd fallen in love with renewing beloved worn shoes in the heart of Montana. He often asked his customers about the journeys they'd been on while wearing their boots, moccasins, dress shoes, or sandals. He lived vicariously through their explorations, making the mending process a journey in itself. Breathing new life into the adventure-filled soles was his passion, prolonging the spirit within each pair. Since his craft presented him with wealthy customers and a steady income, Marty lived comfortably, and mostly at home.

His shop was a walkable distance from his bungalow, which held a fireplace and a library stashed with reckless stories of sacrifice, abandon, and free will. He had a safe space, both at work and at home, and never felt the need to venture out other than to delight in the local restaurants and tearooms. His purpose for shoveling driveways was twofold—it helped bring in extra cash for the trip, but more so, it allowed Marty to practice exploring new places with unknown people.

But it was finally time for him to go on his own adventure rather than reading about one, awakening him from his Montana slumber. Now, the views of the clouds eased his mind. They were dreamlike, relaxing him to a merely physical state of sleep. The four-hour nap was just what he needed, since he hadn't slept much the night before due to a combination of nerves and the last-minute decision to craft something to add to Phoebe's gift. The landing seemed less significant than the takeoff, maybe because Marty was suddenly filled with excitement to meet his niece.

The shoe prints from Marty's boots lined his sister's driveway as he thought about the phone call that got him here, so far from home.

Norvi had moved out when she was eighteen and in love. Alex had stolen her heart, and with his first job taking him to Illinois, Norvi saw no choice but to leave and change her name from Winthrop to Winkler. Their father had expected her to become Marty's assistant in the family business, but her opposing free spirit had other plans. They hadn't spoken in years, and Marty was starting to feel nervous as he approached her home. He knew his niece had been born, but having never left the state of Montana, and his sister not seeing the need to visit after their parents passed, he had yet to meet her.

His glove-covered fist connected with the front door of his sister's house three times, the knocks reverberating throughout the unfamiliar home. He could see Norvi's face morphed by the privacy windowpane on the door.

"Marty! You made it!" she exclaimed as she emerged, hugging her brother more emphatically than he'd expected, the snow trailing through their hair. "Come in, come in!" she said, shivering.

Alex walked into the foyer just as Marty shut the door behind him and rolled his luggage to the side. "Marty, it's been such a long time," he said, opening his arms.

"Hey, Al," Marty responded, happily surprised by another warm greeting.

"She's in by the tree." Alex noticed Marty's expectant gaze as he motioned to the living room.

As he walked through to the next room, he was enthralled by the tree's beauty and twinkling lights, the only source lighting the space. With the leather stockings he'd made years ago hanging on the mantel and the festive decorations carefully placed throughout, the room felt reminiscent of their parents' house at Christmas. His eyes traced over an old family photo on an end table next to the couch when he realized he was in the presence of his little niece.

Phoebe, asleep on the couch, seemed equally comforted by the peaceful ambiance and dim light of the tree. The dog that was curled up next to her legs awoke before she did, greeting the uncle with sleep-coated barks and excited whimpers.

Phoebe rubbed her eyes as she sat up, slowly awakening with the commotion. Making eye contact for the first time, Marty looked at Phoebe, taking in her face, mirroring that of his sister's. She blinked a few times, and just as Marty opened his mouth to introduce himself, a smile overtook her face. Its crooked nature reminded him of his own.

"You're my Uncle Marty!" she squealed as she jumped up from the couch and hugged his legs. "You're a lot taller than my mom!" she said, looking at the man she'd only heard about and seen in photos until now.

Marty squatted down to her level and opened his arms. "Here," he said. "Now I can hug you back."

She rushed into his arms with a giggle. When she pulled away, Marty reached for his shoulder bag, unlatching it to reveal his gift. "Phoebe, I wanted to bring you a Christmas gift," he said. "Now, it's not much, but I want you to know, it's very special."

Phoebe slowly reached out her hands, taking the oddly shaped wrapped package from him. She looked at her parents, who offered her encouraging smiles, and she sat next to the tree to open it. She was very careful, tearing small pieces off at a time. Marty held his breath until finally the dwarf was revealed. Phoebe gasped, her eyebrows creasing in what looked like fear and confusion.

"Don't be frightened. He might look a little different than your other toys, but this is an extraordinary dwarf," Marty said, inching closer to her by the tree.

Phoebe looked at her uncle, her face unchanging before shifting her sight back to the dwarf in her hands.

Sitting next to her now, Marty put his hand under hers. "You see his ears?" he asked. Phoebe nodded. "One is bigger than the other. Normally, dwarves have ears that match, but this one doesn't, and that's what makes him special. Some say he may even be magical."

With that last word, Phoebe looked up into her uncle's eyes, a little spark of wonder igniting.

"Well, his ears and his shoes," Marty corrected. "You see, I make shoes for people. Sometimes they even bring me their old shoes that have holes in them for me to fix. I mend them so they can go do amazing things like climb mountains, march for freedom, and explore the world," he paused, making sure his niece was still interested. Her thumb traced over the leather shoes Marty had added to the dwarf with adhesive while the family dog nudged his way in, sniffing the new, strange toy. "I thought red leather shoes sounded like something not only a special Christmas dwarf would wear, but something a very special niece would wear, too."

With that, Marty rummaged in his bag once more, pulling out a matching pair for Phoebe. She carefully set down the dwarf, her crooked smile returning as she took the shoes from her uncle.

"Will you put them on, Mama?" she asked Norvi.

"Of course," her mother said, tightening the laces before tying them in little bows. "They're perfect, Marty. Thank you." Norvi rubbed her brother's shoulder, an affection he wasn't used to, stirring up unexpected feelings of nostalgia as the three of them sat under the tree together.

"Can I wear them to the ball?" Phoebe asked, her eyes shifting to her dad's.

"Sure, they'll go with your green dress," Alex said, turning his attention to Marty. "I don't know if Norvi mentioned it, but my company is putting on a Yule Ball. I thought it might be fun for all of us to go!"

"Oh, well, I didn't plan to get dressed up. I only brought my day clothes," Marty hesitantly protested as Phoebe watched her feet wiggle in the new shoes under the lights of the tree.

"Not to worry. Al has some dress clothes that would fit you just fine," Norvi said. "It's tonight. Do you think you'll be up for it?" she asked, hope lining her voice.

"I'd love to," Marty said after a deep breath, looking his sister in the eyes, wondering why he'd waited so long to feel the love of family again. It surprised him how much he'd missed her, forgotten memories of camaraderie and laughter suddenly resurfacing.

Phoebe raced up the stairs to her bedroom to get changed for the ball. Her velvet green dress lay on her bed, freshly pressed, waiting for her. She set down her new toy beside it and picked up the dress, turning to study herself in the mirror. She thought about what her uncle said, about how she was a special niece.

Am I really that special? she thought as she looked from the dress to herself. She smiled at her reflection, a dimple appearing on one side of her face. She quickly adjusted her lips back to a straight line, remembering the cruel things her classmates had said to her: that her face was misshapen, that dimples only show up on the faces of "weirdos" and rejects. She looked behind her at the dwarf resting on the comforter and remembered his uneven ears. Phoebe swapped out the dress for the dwarf, looking at him in the mirror next to her. Suddenly, he seemed much cuter than before, with the brilliant blue of his eyes catching her attention.

"If a dwarf with weird ears can be special, then so can I," Phoebe said, the smile and dimple simultaneously returning to her cherub-like face. As she looked at her own reflection, she thought she saw the dwarf nod in agreement out of the corner of her eye.

"Phoebe, it's time to go," she heard her mother yell up the stairs, shoving the previous thought out of Phoebe's mind.

Quickly, she put the dress on over her head and searched deep within her closet. She frantically pulled out shoes, toys, and treasures she'd previously hidden, including rocks from the neighbor's garden, while rummaging. Starting to sweat, she finally saw what she was looking for.

"Here!" she exclaimed, crawling backward out of the closet. "You can come with me tonight!" she said to the dwarf, placing him in a small burlap shoulder bag before heading down the stairs to join the rest of her family. He didn't quite fit in the small pouch; his hat poked through the opening.

"You look beautiful," Uncle Marty said to Phoebe.

Her mother looked at her daughter. "Phoebe, how did you get all sweaty?" Her mother's amused eyes moved to the bag thrown over her shoulder. "And why are you taking that bag? Playing Santa tonight?"

"It's my special purse for tonight. I thought it looked pretty with my dress," Phoebe bluffed, covering it as best she could with her coat, knowing that her mother wouldn't allow her to take the dwarf any other way.

Her mom looked from Uncle Marty back to Phoebe, and Phoebe knew then that her mother had decided not to fight her on this one, probably since it was a special occasion. They might get a few odd looks from people at the ball, but her uncle was here, and that mattered more than arguing over whether Phoebe could bring the bag.

The four of them left the house and began to walk down the street, the snow falling around them as they headed for the L train. It wasn't too far from the house, and while cold, the evening presented a magical undertone accentuated by the snowfall. Phoebe's new red shoes looked quite bright against the white ground. She watched the white flakes dot them as she held Uncle Marty's hand. When she tripped on an uneven wedge in the sidewalk covered by snow, Marty squeezed her hand tighter, keeping her from falling.

"Close one!" she said, beaming up at him when her bag started to shift. She pulled it to the front of her, noticing that now the dwarf's hat and eyes were peering over the edge of the bag.

"Get back in there," she whispered, worried that he'd fall onto the sidewalk like she almost had. She gently pushed him back down, but it felt like he was pushing against her. She looked down again and, with a wink, he slid down into the bag. She gasped.

"You okay, honey?" her dad asked, turning to see Uncle Marty and Phoebe walking a few paces behind.

"Yeah," she said. "I was just looking at the church lights over there!" she exclaimed, trying to deflect.

"They are breathtaking," her dad said, taking in the scene for himself.

The family made it to the train, the busy city streets bustling with people going from this holiday festivity to that family gathering. Marty gripped Phoebe's hand tighter as the crowd grew. It was all Phoebe could do to keep up. She felt like she was going to start flying if her feet moved any faster, the red shoes now a blur. Suddenly, her bag shifted again. She tried to peek at the dwarf, but she had to look ahead to keep up with her parents. A few people pushed past her, brushing against her bag. She couldn't be sure if the dwarf was moving or if it was her imagination, but suddenly her bag seemed lighter. Phoebe slid her hand under her coat to check. It was empty. Out of the corner of her eye, she saw it. The dwarf had jumped from her bag! He was suddenly moving like he was alive.

Without a second thought, Phoebe let go of Uncle Marty's hand. Her eyes were glued on the dwarf as he stuck the landing. He looked back at her, motioning for her to follow him as his tiny legs moved quickly, forcing Phoebe into a jog. He turned a corner, the street opening up to a display of trees, lights perfectly tangled in their branches. Phoebe could see she was going to catch up to him, so she slowed her pace to take in the scene. The dwarf stopped close to the grassy area that housed leafless birches as she took a step next to him, away from the bustling sidewalks. He reached up and placed his tiny ceramic hand in hers as they watched the lights twinkle.

"You're alive," she said, beginning to kneel to the dwarf's level, the same way her uncle had when they'd met earlier that evening.

The dwarf nodded. Phoebe watched intently as he smiled at her, putting his hand to her dimple. She put her hand on top of his, unbelieving that she'd made such an unusual friend. The dwarf lifted his other hand, extending one finger. Phoebe followed his gaze to a nearby bench where a woman was sitting alone. She looked back at the dwarf, who put his hand on his chest where his heart would be.

"What is it?" Phoebe asked. She barely got out the words when a tall woman dressed for what could be a Christmas party at the Ritz-Carlton almost tripped over her.

"Oh! I'm sorry. I didn't see you there, honey. Are you okay?" the woman asked.

Phoebe looked down at the dwarf who had stiffened, standing motionless like when she'd unwrapped him, except now he had one finger over his mouth, exemplifying a shush. She uttered the words, "I think so." The fashionable woman stood there a while longer for her own reassurance before hurrying off.

Phoebe looked quizzically at the dwarf as he began motioning again, now frantically. She wondered why he'd stopped when the woman came by, thinking her mind was starting to play tricks on her. He was moving after all—a toy come to life.

The dwarf wrapped his arms around one of Phoebe's legs in a hug and then pointed back to the bench. He did this a couple of times before she understood.

"You want to hug that woman?" Phoebe's wandering thoughts subdued, replaced by the urgency coming from her unlikely Christmas present. The dwarf shook his head and pointed at Phoebe, hugged her leg once more, then pointed at the bench.

"You want *me* to go hug her?" she asked, her voice louder and lined with confusion. The dwarf nodded and began to gently push her in that direction.

"But I don't know her," Phoebe said, staying put. She picked up the dwarf and held him in her hands, admiring his sweet nature. He put one of his little hands on hers and smiled at her. Even though his glass-like hands were hard, she could feel the warmth of his heart. She hugged him before setting him back down. "I think you're my favorite Christmas present."

The toy held her gaze for a moment, their matching joy reflected in each other's expressions, before he tried his best to push her toward the bench again, but Phoebe wouldn't budge. So instead, he took off running in the direction of the woman.

"Wait!" Phoebe screamed, chasing after him. She tried to catch up, but not before the dwarf was swiftly kicked by a city walker. The sound of broken glass erupted in Phoebe's ears. "No!"

She ran over to what used to be her dwarf. She meekly picked up his pieces, tears stinging the backs of her eyes. She could hear her name in the not-too-far-off distance, but she couldn't be sure with her quickened heartbeat reverberating through her ears.

"Phoebe?" It was getting louder now with each syllable drawn out. "Phoebe, where are you?"

Uncle Marty was suddenly beside her. "Phoebe! I thought I'd lost you! What happened?" he asked, confused.

"The dwarf jumped out of my bag," Phoebe said, wiping away a tear. She heard someone else crying, too. She looked up to see the woman the dwarf had motioned to, all alone on the bench. The only companion she had was a dog sitting next to her, which looked a lot like Phoebe's dog. Phoebe paused in her own sad state before she took the broken dwarf in her hands and walked over to the woman.

"Phoebe, where are you going?" Uncle Marty asked, briskly following her.

"What's wrong?" Phoebe asked the woman.

"Oh, hello, sweetheart. I'm okay," the woman said, trying to control her sobs.

"But you're crying," Phoebe pried.

"Well, my son wasn't able to come home for Christmas. I couldn't wait to see his bright blue eyes, those eyes that have so much love in them, and now I'll have to wait until next year." She paused to wipe away a stream of tears. "I decided to take a walk to get my mind off of it, but I couldn't see because I couldn't stop crying. So I thought I'd take a break here and get all the sadness out before I started again."

Phoebe felt sad, too. Not only for her broken dwarf, but now also for the woman who wouldn't get to see her son. This must be why the dwarf so badly wanted Phoebe to give her a hug. She looked down at her beloved toy and noticed a portion of his broken face that showed a blue eye. She picked up the piece of porcelain and handed it to the woman.

The woman reached down to meet Phoebe's small hand. "What's this?" she asked.

"It's a beautiful blue eye," Phoebe said, her heart suddenly beating quickly, as if applauding her, and an overwhelming sense of love filled her.

"Oh my," the woman said, looking past the piece of dwarf directly at Phoebe. "Dear, you look radiant," she said.

Phoebe smiled and pulled at the ends of her dress, ready to explain to her that they were headed to a ball, but then she saw that her dress was sparkling. It was as if a thousand diamonds had been added to it.

"Phoebe! What are you doing?" her mother asked as she ran toward the bench with her father trailing right behind her.

"We thought we lost you!" her dad exclaimed as Uncle Marty and Phoebe turned to meet them.

"I found her. Everything's okay," Uncle Marty comforted her mom, which looked oddly easy. "We had an accident with the dwarf," he said, but his eyes never left Phoebe.

"So, that's what was in the bag . . . Listen, I'm so sorry about the dwarf, Marty. But the ball is about to start. Come on, let's get to the train," her mom said, taking one of Phoebe's hands into her own.

Phoebe shoved the remains of her dwarf into her burlap sack as they headed back toward the train. She had meant to hug the woman as the dwarf had wished, but thought his eye had done just as much as a hug would have, maybe even more. She longed for him to come back to life, saddened by a friendship that had ended before it had truly started.

"Merry Christmas, sweetheart!" the woman from the bench yelled, admiring the odd gift given to her by a stranger. Phoebe waved at the woman with her one free hand before she was out of sight, immersed into the crowded streets.

The train always felt much faster to Phoebe than the actual pace at which it was moving. She watched out the window as the snow blew past, looking more like lines of white than individual flakes, the speed tricking her eyes to see a blizzard rather than a gentle, steady snowfall.

"Uncle Marty! Watch!" she yelled, even though her uncle was sitting directly next to her. He turned his attention to her as she exhaled onto the window, creating a cloud of breath that she drew a snowman onto with her finger.

"You're a pretty impressive artist," Uncle Marty said as she giggled. He tapped her dimple. "Hey, we have the same smile," he said, pointing to his own dimple that only appeared when he showcased the widest of grins.

Phoebe hung her head. "It's not a good smile."

Uncle Marty lifted her chin to meet his eyes. "Who told you that?"

"Some people at school. They said only ugly people have dimples." She sat there playing with her gloves in her lap when she quickly turned her uncle in realization. "Hey, but you're not ugly," she said, studying him.

"Whoever said that was probably just jealous that your smile is so cute. Dimples add character; they add something interesting to your face. Not everyone has them, which makes them special."

"I like that we match," Phoebe said.

"You know, we also have last names that start with the same letter," Uncle Marty added.

"Your name starts with a W, too?" Phoebe yelled in disbelief.

"Yep! Winthrop. Your mom's name used to be that, too, until she married your dad."

Phoebe nodded with a thoughtful expression, feeling the crunch of ceramic from the broken dwarf in her bag. Her mind wandered back to the sad moment, before she realized that Uncle Marty was there to witness it. "Uncle Marty, did you notice the dwarf earlier? Did you see him move?" Phoebe was whispering now.

"Phoebe, I'm sorry, I didn't see him move. I was terrified trying to find you. Then, I heard you scream, and that's when I saw him, shattered on the sidewalk."

"Well, I think he was alive. Earlier, I even saw him wink at me."

"When was this?" Uncle Marty amused her.

"When I tripped on the sidewalk. I looked down to make sure he was still tucked in my bag, and his eyes were out, like he was watching where we were going. Before I pushed him back inside my bag, he winked at me."

"Wow! Well, I knew he was an extraordinary dwarf. I guess I just didn't know how extraordinary," Uncle Marty said.

As Phoebe sat pondering her dwarf and replaying the wink, she started to wonder again if she imagined the whole thing, but she remembered the feeling of him hugging her leg. A little saddened, she focused her attention back to the blizzard-like snow when a small sound came from under her seat. She folded in half to look below and noticed that her bag had slid off and started to move backward with the motion of the train. It had fallen two seats behind them. Panicked, she got up from her seat to grab it.

"I'll be right back," she said to Uncle Marty, who nodded.

Once out of his sight, Phoebe got on her hands and knees to find her bag. It had shifted farther back by two more seats. Finally, it stopped, the handle catching on a metal pole of a chair. She quickly hopped to her feet and ran to its location.

"Excuse me," she said to a young boy about her age sitting in the seat her bag was under. "My bag is under your chair. It slid down the train," she said.

The boy, unsure, folded over and saw the burlap bag resting under his chair in between his worn-through dress shoes. "Here it is!" he yelled. As he pulled it out from under the seat, a piece of the dwarf fell into his lap.

"Here you go," he hesitantly said, looking down at the broken leg and red shoe. He picked it up with his other hand, examining it. "Uh, what's this?" he asked.

"That's a piece of my Christmas present from my uncle. He brought me a magical dwarf, and he makes shoes, so he put new ones on it. But he broke."

"Your uncle makes shoes? So does my dad!"

"Whoa, really?"

"Well, he did. He died last year. These shoes actually remind me of some he made for my sister," the boy said, lowering his head, rubbing the red leather shoe for comfort.

Phoebe studied him. Remembering how much the dwarf meant to the woman on the bench, she replied, "Why don't you keep it?"

"What?" The boy's eyes lit up.

"I know it's kind of a weird gift, being a broken leg and all, but maybe it can remind you of your dad and the beautiful shoes he made."

"Wow, thanks," he said, admiring the little shoe, then directing his attention back to Phoebe. "Was your hair like that before?" he asked.

Phoebe looked at the window, seeing her faint, but breathtaking reflection. Her hair was no longer straight and resting at her shoulders, but in a bun with curls tracing her face.

"Whoa," she whispered as the boy quizzically watched her.

"Phoebe, is that you?" her dad called a few seats farther back, looking at her curiously, like he couldn't tell what was different.

"Hey, Dad!" she said.

"Why aren't you in your seat with Uncle Marty?"

"My bag got lost, so I had to find it," she said as her dad walked to meet her.

"Come on, let's get you back to your seat. You can't just wander around on a train; it can be dangerous," he warned.

Phoebe glanced one last time at the boy, who was handing over the dwarf's leg with the little red shoe to whom she assumed was his sister. The small girl giggled while studying it. Phoebe smiled, but before she moved back to her seat, she noticed the boy take off one of his own shoes. It was no longer tattered and old, but shiny and new. He followed Phoebe's line of sight as they looked at each other, sharing in the mysterious magic of the moment.

Feeling extra confident with her sparkly dress and fancy hair, Marty could tell Phoebe was excited for the ball. She held his hand as they entered the grand ballroom. Strings of lights hung from the ceiling, wrapped around columns, and twinkled across the floor, the reflection making those who were dancing appear to be floating.

Marty felt his hand warm in hers. "Uncle Marty, your hand is a bit clammy," she said, slowly removing hers from it.

Marty smiled down at her, but not with a smile that sported his dimple. It was a brief grin that quickly made its way back to a straight face posture. Marty watched a beautiful woman from across the room beaming while she talked with those around her.

Following his gaze, Phoebe dug into her bag, sifting through the broken remains of her dwarf. "Here," she said. Instead of holding Marty's hand, she placed the little dwarf's hand into his.

"What's this for?" Marty asked.

"Uncle Marty, you gave me a magical dwarf. Now that he's broken, he's making other people happy. I think his secret is that you have to give him away to someone else."

Marty listened to her six-year-old reasoning.

"I think if you give his hand to someone who needs it, he'll give you something you want, too," she said, looking back at the beautiful woman he had been admiring.

"Phoebe, that's very generous of you, but I'm not sure who would want a broken dwarf hand," he said, shifting his gaze to his sister, who was off by herself while Al talked with his coworkers. She seemed uninterested or possibly subdued. It was Christmas Eve, and Marty didn't understand why she wouldn't be bursting at the seams with the excitement she annually expressed up until the day she left Montana.

Not to mention, they'd finally made it to the ball, after all.

"Maybe you have a point," he reconsidered. "I'll be right back." He left Phoebe next to Alex, thumbing the tiny dwarf hand in his.

Marty asked a question he hadn't asked his sister since they were kids. "Are you doing okay?" Norvi had always been independent, proving her strength at any chance she could when they were teenagers.

"Marty, I don't understand."

"Don't understand what, Norvi?"

"How it's taken us this long to reunite."

Marty paused, saddened by the distance and silence they'd allowed into their lives. "I mean this in the best way possible," he paused. "I didn't realize how much I missed you."

Norvi laughed.

"And to answer your question, I don't think either of us saw getting together as a necessity. I know we're family, but we're also really strong people by ourselves. We know how to survive on our own. Our parents instilled that within us, you know?"

"I know. You're right. I just didn't realize how much I'd missed you either. I knew Phoebe would love you, but seeing how much she loves you—the way she's quick to hold your hand, how she rushes to be near you, and how she looks at you like you're already familiar—makes me wish I'd kept in touch."

"Me too," Marty said, slowly opening his hand, presenting her with the tiny hand of the dwarf. "Take this. Set it somewhere you'll see every so often. Then, when you do, give me a call or write to me. It'll be a reminder. I may not be around to give you a hand, but I'd like to lend my ear."

Norvi grinned, audibly laughing at the ridiculous yet meaningful gesture. "I'm sorry Phoebe broke your gift," she said, taking it from him.

"That's okay. I didn't expect her to find so much joy in it. Oddly, I think she might like it better now that it's broken," he said, chuckling.

"Here," Norvi said as she pulled a bobby pin from her hair. "This can be your reminder to do the same for me."

Marty nodded, placing the pin in his pocket when he felt a tap on his shoulder. He turned around, suddenly face to face with the woman he'd seen earlier.

"Hi, I'm Maria. Would you like to dance?" she asked.

Marty introduced himself as he confidently walked her to the center of the room. The start of the next song began, and he moved with ease like he'd never done before. He felt like one of the main characters in his books: a strong man who climbed mountains, founded cities, and fell in love. As he twirled Maria, he saw Phoebe out of the corner of his eye. She winked at him before looking back at her mom, who was studying the little hand of the dwarf.

When the last song played, Alex, Norvi, Phoebe, and Marty all gathered together to dance as a family. They spun each other, laughter filling their lungs. As the song came to a close, little Phoebe pulled on Marty's coattails. He bent down as she whispered, "If this is what Christmas Eve is like with an uncle, I can't wait for tomorrow."

Christmas morning was filled with the scent of sweet bread, the sound of Phoebe's laughter interspersed with holiday tunes, and feelings of joy. Suddenly, time moved by too quickly, and Marty was packed to head back home.

After his last goodbyes, he shut the door behind him and stood on the porch. Marty took a moment and looked down at his shoes, the shoes that had once only seen his town in Montana—the shop where he worked, nearby cafés, and libraries. Now, they'd been to an entirely different state and on several adventures with his niece. He couldn't wait until next year, when he'd promised himself and her to take multiple trips to see her, becoming more like his books, his customers, and the person he longed to be. His next steps felt different as they led him to the car that was waiting to take him to the airport.

Marty had nearly missed his plane due to the ample amount of goodbye hugs he'd given to Phoebe, happily pushing his departure to the last minute. Quickly showing the attendant his boarding pass, it was time for his second flight. He knew this one would be different from the first, not just because he was headed back home, but because he recognized a beautiful woman seated on the left, looking out the window, whose name would never escape him.

One Year Later...

"Oh, Marty! Come on in!" Norvi said, swinging the door wide as she made her way back into the house through the chaos. She had promised Phoebe's class choir lessons at her house, the last lesson falling on Christmas Eve, the day of their big show. Phoebe hadn't had a group of friends like this over to the house before, but her newfound dwarf-granted confidence had her surrounded with them this school year. Marty was excited about the new adventure the family would embark upon this season, now including another member—Maria. Phoebe ran past Uncle Marty, tripping on his suitcase and quickly uttering an apology as she rushed to help her mother.

Marty was surprised his niece didn't greet him like usual on his quarterly visits when she paused and slowly walked back to where he was standing. She looked at his bearded face—the stubble had grown quickly over the last few months—and blinked, recognition suddenly sweeping across her face.

"Oh, I know you. Merry Christmas, Uncle Marty!" she exclaimed, jumping into his arms.

With most of the dwarf given away, Phoebe stood taller, looked more mature somehow, but still fit perfectly in Marty's embrace.

"Uncle Marty, I want to show you something." She dug into the pocket of her dress, pulling out the last remaining piece of the dwarf, a piece of his face containing one of his bright blue eyes.

Marty reached down as she placed it in his hand, her small hand tracing its outline. The single eye winked, a simultaneous gasp filling both Marty and his niece with wonder as they looked at the broken, magical Christmas dwarf.

About the Author

Nat Bickel is an energetic writer who moves people to action with her words with bylines in the *Los Angeles Times*, *PopSugar*, *Glamour*, *Darling Magazine*, and more. She's also the author of the books *The Catalyst*, *The Christmas Clue*, and *The Volcano No One Could See*. When she's not writing, you can find her taking film photos, pressing flowers, or blazing new trails with her husband.

You can find Nat across all socials at:
@natmosfear

To learn more about Nat, visit her website at:
https://www.natmosfear.com

Back in Shape

Back in Shape

Cheryl Boughton

"I can't believe I'm missing the Christmas dance for this," my sister muttered, staring out the car window as slush hissed beneath the tires. "All my friends are going. I'm the odd one out. Isn't this the season of giving? Why wasn't I given a pass on this?"

"I've had enough of your griping, young lady," Mom said, eyes fixed on the highway ahead. "It's bad enough your father's back is acting up. We don't need your complaining to add to the stress."

"I still don't see why I had to come," Michelle pressed. "If you just told them I had somewhere else to be, they'd have understood."

"We hardly ever see them," Mom snapped. "We're going, and we're going to have a good time. End of conversation."

Silence settled over the car. Michelle sulked. Dad dozed in the passenger seat, having downed the maximum dose of over-the-counter painkillers before we left.

The cars flashed past as we made our way along the Queen Elizabeth Way toward my aunt and uncle's house for our annual pre-Christmas get-together—a triple-duty celebration for my birthday, my uncle's birthday, and Christmas itself. The trunk was crammed with wrapped gifts, and between me and Michelle sat a veggie platter, the only healthy item likely to appear on tonight's menu. Every lane change made the carrot and celery sticks tremble like nervous passengers.

Uncle Henry and Aunt Evelyn were good, God-fearing people—not in the "See you at Christmas Eve service" way, but in the full-time, twenty-four-seven, "The Lord has a plan for everything, including why your toast lands butter-side up" way. They were also my godparents, which meant my soul was, in theory, their responsibility. They took it seriously.

Every visit came with what I called The Burning Question. The wording varied, but the point never did:

"Deborah, is your name written in the Book of Life?"

Or,

"Deborah, does Jesus, our Lord and Savior, know your name?"

By the time I was ten, I knew the drill: say yes, smile like you are one of the saved, and move on. Michelle was never asked The Burning Question, which I felt was completely unfair. She liked to joke they'd written her off as a lost cause long ago.

I had five cousins, all older than me and my sister. In addition to their work or educational commitments, they traveled around the world as The Heavenly Seven, the missing two being my aunt and uncle. They toured in an enormous beige motorhome that my sister and I secretly called The Immaculate Contraption. We'd heard the stories—how the brakes failed in Sudbury but the Lord, in His infinite timing, provided an uphill slope; or how a wheel came off in Saskatchewan yet rolled, guided, my aunt insisted, by the unmistakable hand of God, neatly into a service station. Personally, I always wondered why the same hand didn't just keep the wheel on in the first place.

The memory faded as the car hit a patch of slush, pulling me back to the here and now. Michelle had stopped complaining out loud, but every sigh and exaggerated head turn toward the frosted window was its own adolescent performance piece. Dad's occasional wince or soft grunt reminded me that we were heading into this evening with a fragile spine in the passenger seat and a volatile mood in the back. The veggie platter continued to wobble between us, the fat-free ranch dip threatening to slosh over the edge. Somewhere ahead, my aunt and uncle's house—and The Burning Question—waited.

The tires crunched over the icy driveway, the headlights sweeping across the snowbanks piled high along the edges. Through the frost-speckled windshield, the house glowed like a beacon: every window lit, wreath on the door, and a twinkle of Christmas lights strung neatly along the eaves. A plastic nativity scene stood in the yard, the Magi forever mid-journey through a drift of snow.

Mom eased the car into a spot beside The Immaculate Contraption, its sides plastered with decals from places near and far. Before we'd even opened our doors, the warm smell of woodsmoke drifted out to greet us.

We tumbled out into the cold, our breath puffing in white clouds. The gifts were redistributed—Mom with the veggie platter, Michelle with the stack of smaller packages, me balancing an awkwardly wrapped board game—and we shuffled toward the front steps, boots squeaking on the packed snow.

The door opened before we could knock, and Aunt Evelyn's voice rang out: "Well, look who's here!" She wrapped me in a hug that smelled faintly of Shalimar perfume and oven heat. Uncle Henry was right behind her, grinning like we'd just made his week.

The moment we stepped inside, the warmth hit us full in the face, carrying the unmistakable scent of ham and scalloped potatoes. From deeper inside came the sounds of clinking cutlery and the low hum of voices—and somewhere, unmistakably, the deep, warm chords of their electric organ. My cousin David was playing, fingers gliding over the keys with an ease that made even the simplest carol sound like a cathedral performance. The music threaded through the air like an extra ribbon on the evening, tying everything together.

Cousins bustled past with platters and tea towels, pausing for quick hugs before disappearing again.

The house was as much a statement of faith as it was of family—the Christmas tree, heavy with decades of ornaments; a wooden nativity scene on the sideboard; gold-framed Bible verses on the hallway wall; and photographs from The Heavenly Seven's travels: Henry in a cowboy hat in Alberta, Evelyn greeting a missionary in Ghana, all seven smiling stiffly in matching powder-blue blazers at the Grand Canyon.

"Coats in the front room, girls," Evelyn called, already turning back toward the kitchen where laughter and clinking cutlery mingled with the scent of yeast. Mom's gaze swept over the table, already laden with ham, potatoes, salads drenched in mayonnaise and cheesy casseroles, and I could almost hear the mental Jazzercise math ticking in her head. She'd be working this off until at least mid-January.

We all found our seats as Uncle Henry cleared his throat, a familiar cue. Heads bowed, some reverently, others out of habit, as he offered a prayer of thanks for the food, the family gathered around it, and "safe travels for those still on the road." His deep voice rolled into a verse of "Praise God, from Whom All Blessings Flow," and soon the whole table joined in, the harmony well-rehearsed from years of repetition.

When the final "Amen" faded, serving spoons clinked against dishes and the dining room table truly came into its own, groaning under the weight of Aunt Evelyn's Christmas spread. The glazed ham gleamed under the chandelier light, ringed with pineapple slices and cherries. Beside it sat a bubbling dish of oily scalloped potatoes, vegetables cooked until they surrendered entirely, and our lone contribution—the neatly arranged veggie platter with a tub of fat-free ranch. My mother made a point of starting with a carrot stick and three broccoli flowerets.

Everyone knew that my mother was an excellent cook and took nutrition seriously which, in the 1980s, meant everything was fat-free. Skim milk. Low-fat yogurt. Margarine instead of butter. Meals in our house came with vegetables that still had a bit of crunch and desserts that were portioned with restraint. At Aunt Evelyn's, it was the polar opposite. Cooking wasn't really her forte, and nutrition never made it to the table. The vegetables were boiled into submission, the potatoes were swimming in cream, and the ham was lacquered with enough brown sugar to make your teeth ache. Everyone piled their plates high—not just full, but leaning-tower full—as if the real miracle of Christmas was seeing just how much food you could balance on one piece of china.

Conversation at my aunt and uncle's table was always lively but carefully scrubbed clean of anything impolite. My cousins never swore; the worst they'd call each other was "armpit" or "toenail," which, to my mind, wasn't much better than using other body parts. No one ever said "Oh my God," either. They would never take the Lord's name in vain. I'd trained myself to turn God into "gosh" mid-syllable if I slipped up, like swerving to avoid a pothole.

Between bites, the talk began to drift, as it always did, toward testimonies and travel tales—the miracle stories from The Heavenly Seven were as much a part of the meal as the ham and potatoes. You could count on at least one involving a near disaster on the road, another about divine intervention in the nick of time, all shared with the quiet conviction of people for whom faith wasn't just belief, but the lens through which the entire world made sense.

I'd grown up with a father who was both a man of faith and a man of science, the sort who could believe in God while still knowing that brakes give out because of physics, not the Devil, and that a rolling wheel in Saskatchewan was more about gravity than divine guidance. So, while I nodded and smiled in the right places, part of me wondered if some of these miracles might have been helped along by aerodynamics, tire tread, or just dumb luck. In my cousins' world, questioning a miracle was a serious matter—not unlike using the Lord's name carelessly. It was part of the unspoken code: you could laugh and tease about plenty of things, but faith and its workings were never among them.

But that night, there was a new testimony. My cousin Sarah leaned forward, eyes alight. "And remember the *river* in Kenya? We were meant to cross at the main bridge, but Dad felt the Lord telling him to go upstream. Well, wouldn't you know, the bridge collapsed less than an hour later! We'd have been right on it if we hadn't listened to the message." Heads around the table nodded solemnly, murmuring "Praise God" like punctuation.

Midway through my second helping of potatoes, Uncle Henry set down his fork and fixed me with his familiar, unwavering gaze.

"Deborah," he asked, "are you saved?"

"Yes," I said, delivering my standard answer with the practiced smile I'd perfected years ago.

But he didn't look away. His eyes stayed on me, patient, expectant.

Worried there was going to be a precedent-setting second *Burning Question*, I quickly added, "Praise be to God."

Only then did he nod, satisfied, and turn back to his plate. Across the table, Michelle caught my eye and smirked into her glass of apple juice.

Dessert was just as much of an event: a chocolate Yule log swirled with cream, a dense, dark Christmas cake (no booze, of course, this was a teetotal house), and a platter piled high with sugar-dusted shortbread, jam thumbprints, and intricately piped cookies from their church's annual cookie walk. The sweet smell of cinnamon, chocolate, and almond hung in the air as everyone lingered around the table, trading one last round of stories before the plates were finally cleared.

As if we hadn't eaten enough, Aunt Evelyn disappeared into the kitchen and returned with two cakes: one with pink rosettes spelling *Happy Birthday, Deborah*, the other iced in blue with *Happy Birthday, Henry*. His birthday was the day before mine, and every year we shared this moment like a duet: two candles, two choruses, one long family tradition. He was fifty-five that year; I'd just turned eighteen. We made a strange pair, but the good will was genuine.

Michelle leaned toward me and whispered, "Does this mean we're about to get the prettiest 'Happy Birthday' in the province?"

This year, David slid from the table to the electric organ, flexed his fingers, and gave a playful little run up the keys. Everyone stood, chairs scraping back, and launched into "Happy Birthday." But in this house, it wasn't the mumbled, off-key version you hear at restaurants. It was . . . glorious. Years of singing in church choirs and on gospel tours poured into that song, voices blending in perfect harmony. My cousins' sopranos floated above my aunt's steady alto, while Uncle Henry anchored the bass like he was laying the foundation for a hymn. Even "Happy Birthday" sounded like something you'd stand for in church.

Michelle caught my eye over the candles and mouthed the word *wow*. She wasn't wrong. It was the most beautiful "Happy Birthday" I'd ever heard.

"Since we're in good voice . . ." Aunt Evelyn said, and David segued effortlessly into "O Come, All Ye Faithful." The carols rolled one after another, each organ chord filling the dining room, the sound swelling so big it seemed to press against the walls. Each carol was more polished than the last, complete with harmonies, swelling dynamics, and the occasional dramatic flourish. From "Hark! The Herald Angels Sing" to "Silent Night," they sang like people who believed every word—and could hit every note. The sound filled the dining room until it felt almost too small to contain it. Michelle, who had refused to sing a single note in public, was actually mouthing along to "Angels We Have Heard on High."

When the final *heavenly peace* of "Silent Night" faded into the clink of tea-cups, Aunt Evelyn clasped her hands together and said, "Now, wasn't that lovely? Time for presents!" And just like that, the music dissolved into the rustle of wrapping paper being fetched from under the tree.

We all shuffled into the living room, the air still warm from the woodstove, the scent of pine mixing with candle wax. In my aunt and uncle's house, Christmas gifts almost always came wrapped in shiny paper from the church bazaar and contained something faith-based—a Christian paperback with a title like *A Voice in the Wind*, a framed scripture verse done in delicate calligraphy, or a piece of art featuring lambs looking up at a distant light. Michelle leaned close again and whispered, "Place your bets: do you think we'll get something with a sheep or a shepherd this year?"

One of my cousins handed my mother a small, flat package. Inside was a bookmark, the kind made from stiff plastic mesh where you thread colored yarn through the square holes. This particular bookmark was done in brown with a blue background, the negative space forming a single word.

I could see it instantly—JESUS—like a neon sign in my brain. But my mother tilted her head, smiling politely.

"Oh, that's beautiful stitching," she said.

"They worked hard on it," Aunt Evelyn said, beaming. "Can you see what it says?"

For the life of her, my mother just couldn't read the word.

I stage-whispered from the couch, "*Jesus*. It says *Jesus*," but Mom didn't seem to hear me. She kept turning it over in her hands, still admiring the handiwork.

"It's so precise. Look how straight the rows are," she offered. "Is this called cross-stitch or embroidery? I'm not sure."

Across the room, one of my cousins leaned forward, their voice just a touch more insistent. "But can you see what it says?"

"Yes, yes, the colors are just lovely," Mom replied, still avoiding the one-word answer they were clearly fishing for. I sat there wondering if my mother had just failed some sort of unspoken test of faith—the kind where only the true believers could read the hidden word. I worried she was about to become a lost cause, like my sister.

Eventually, one of the cousins laughed awkwardly and said, "It says Jesus."

My mother smiled warmly. "Ohhh, yes, of course," she said, nodding. But I wasn't convinced she had seen it for herself.

The gift exchange went on, more books, more inspirational wall art, but that moment stuck with me. In our family, the presents came wrapped in paper and were filled with good intentions. They truly wanted the best for us.

Finally, it was time to leave. We said our thank-yous, gathered our gifts, and headed for the door. My cousins retrieved our coats, and we began bundling up against the cold.

What we had failed to notice is that my father was stuck in his chair in the living room. After an hour in a soft, antique chair, his back had completely given out. After much effort, he stood. He was a most peculiar shape: his hips went one way, his mid-back another, his shoulders the opposite. He looked less like a man and more like a human cursive letter. He was a walking S.

As he slowly made his way to the door, one of my cousins helped him put on his coat. My father winced as the coat slid onto his shoulders. Just then, another cousin, Olivia, said. "We're so sorry your back is bad, Uncle Mark. Would you like us to pray for you?"

My father, assuming they meant they'd keep him in mind later, perhaps at bedtime or at Sunday service, said, "Sure."

They meant *now*. Right now.

Before he could do anything, hands were laid upon him. The room filled with voices, none of it discernable to me. It was no earthly language. They were speaking in tongues, something I had never witnessed before. My mother, Michelle, and I stood there in our winter coats, heat building beneath the wool. We didn't know whether to look at my dad or our boots.

I fixed my eyes on a wooden plaque in the foyer: *God is Love*. I read it once. Then again. *God is Love. God is Love.* I prayed silently, not for my father's back but that my no-nonsense mother wouldn't say something sharp enough to cut through the prayer circle.

One cousin leaned in, eyes bright. "Do you feel something, Uncle Mark? My hand's getting warmer."

Silence. My father didn't answer. *What was he doing?*

My sister shifted her stance. My mother started to stir. I prayed that my father would respond before my typically outspoken mother did.

The moment stretched on. I could hear the grandfather clock ticking in the hallway. My scarf prickled against my neck. My mother inhaled—sharply. I prayed harder: *Please don't let her speak. Please don't let her speak.*

Another cousin said, "Are you sure you don't feel anything Uncle Mark? The Lord is with us."

Finally, my father opened his mouth.

"I feel . . ." he began, then paused just long enough for everyone to lean in closer, "a tingling sensation."

It was the exact line from a Denorex shampoo television commercial that ran every night that winter. Of all the things he could have said in that moment—something pious, something poetic—my father reached for a hair product advertising copy. I've never understood why that was the one phrase his brain decided to serve up, surrounded as he was by praying hands and holy expectation.

I bit the inside of my cheek to keep from laughing. My mother, to my relief, stayed silent.

Then, in what could only be described as an earthly miracle, my father straightened his back, vertebra by vertebra, until he was standing tall and level. He declared himself cured.

"Hallelujah!" they cried.

"Let's go," my mother said.

Without delay, we filed out to the driveway. The cold air hit our faces. And as we climbed into the station wagon, my father's back quietly returned to its previous S-shape.

We'd barely cleared the driveway before Michelle began to snigger.

"So," she said, drawing out the word like a late-night radio host. "Deborah . . . are you saved?"

I groaned. "Oh, stop it."

She grinned. "Because if you'd just given Uncle Henry a *better* answer, maybe we wouldn't have ended up in that prayer ambush in the foyer."

"That's not what triggered it," I said. "It was Mom. If she'd just *seen* the word *Jesus* on that bookmark like a normal person, we'd have been out the door ten minutes earlier."

From the driver's seat, Mom huffed. "I did see it. I just didn't want to say the wrong thing."

Michelle snorted. "The wrong thing? It was literally *Jesus*. There *is* no wrong answer."

"And Dad," I said, "of all the possible responses in the universe, you went with Denorex?"

He shrugged. "It was all I could think of. Plus, I was feeling tingly."

Michelle snorted so hard she nearly choked. "That's it. Next year I'm getting you a bottle for Christmas."

We all laughed—the kind of breathless, can't-stop laugh that makes your stomach hurt. Even Dad was chuckling, though bent once more into his sideways S and wincing when he laughed.

By the time we hit the highway, Michelle wiped her eyes and said, "That was better than any dance I could've gone to."

"The only thing missing," I said, "was our own encore."

Michelle grinned and, without warning, launched into the most exaggerated, off-key "Happy Birthday" I've ever heard, complete with fake operatic flourishes. I joined in, both of us mangling the harmony so badly that Dad was shaking with laughter, even bent into his sideways S.

"Stop, stop," he groaned. "You'll finish me off."

"Don't worry," Michelle said. "If that happens, we know some people who can pray you back."

And as the highway stretched out before us, I realized that what mattered most wasn't the carols or the casseroles or even the burning questions—it was the laughter that carried us home, together, into the heart of winter.

About the Author

Cheryl Boughton is a lifelong reader-turned-writer who loves exploring the quiet corners of family life—the moments where love, doubt, and humor meet. After a long career in education, she's now happily writing stories and essays about belonging and second chances. "Back in Shape" is her first published short story. Cheryl also writes *The Novel Note* on Substack and runs Novel Escapes, in which she creates book-inspired retreats for women. She lives in Kitchener, Ontario, with her husband, David, and their two British Blue cats, Oliver and Poppy.

You can find Cheryl on Instagram:
@cherylboughton

To learn more about Cheryl and Novel Escapes, visit her website at:
https://novelescapes.ca/stories-im-telling

Christmas on
Canal Street

Christmas on Canal Street

Katherine Rea

Megan

As I stand on Canal Street, I stare at the yellow front door of my childhood home. That door was always so cheery, so quirky . . . so forced. Just like my responses to colleagues had been about my plans for Christmas.

"Oh, y'know," I'd said. "Going home for the holidays."

"Ooh, where's home?" they'd ask, inevitably.

"Venice Beach," I'd say with a smile. Inwardly, I'd sigh. In New York, this was hopelessly exotic.

"Ooh must be nice!" they'd chuckle. "No snow for you, eh?"

"Nope," I'd agree, sipping a little more aggressively at my drink. "Just a lot of weed and weirdos."

When did I become so bitter about Venice, I wonder? I used to love it, especially around Christmas. I thought it looked magical, with the lights reflecting off the canals, the odd mix of beachgoers wearing Santa Hats with boardshorts, and palm trees swaying against blue sky as I listened to Frank Sinatra croon about snow and frightful weather.

Yet, I'd done everything I could to get away from my childhood home. Or, so I thought. I'd succeeded in staying away for the last seven years. I hadn't even known my mom was sick. Even though we hadn't been close, I wish I'd known. And Dad had passed so shortly after her, there hadn't even been time to come out and see him either.

I sigh and turn the key in the lock of the yellow door. It's December 22, and I'm tired. My flight out of New York was delayed due to an unexpected snowstorm. But I guess one good thing about being divorced is that you can change your plans on a dime. That, and I don't have to go to my mother-in-law's in upstate New York for Christmas anymore. Thank God.

The entryway is quiet, and my footsteps ring out on the flagstone steps. As with most things, my parents had fallen backward into a goldmine with this house. They'd bought it in 1980, and it had increased at least five times in value. I'd had a quick chat with a realtor before I'd left New York. Even with the minimal maintenance my parents had done over the years, this house was worth upward of two million.

I drop my heavy suitcase in the entryway and look into the open living room in front of me. The bohemian décor is exactly as I remember it, down to my mother's massive self-portrait looming over the fireplace. I'm ready for bed, but first, I want to peek around the rest of the house—at least the first floor. I run my fingers along the wall as I make my way to the kitchen, and that's when I hear a loud rustling, followed by the clang of someone dropping a saucepan.

My whole body tenses, and I feel for my phone in my pocket.

"Who's there?" I call out. I flatten my body along the hallway and edge closer to the kitchen. I see the figure of a man hunched over, facing away from me, illuminated by several camping lights. A squatter? I'm scared, but I feel anger rise in my chest. This was *my* childhood home.

"I know Krav Maga, asshole. And the police are on their way," I yell as I pull out my phone to dial 911.

The figure freezes, but instead of running away, or turning to attack, he stands up and turns around slowly.

"Megan?"

I gasp. "Max? What are you doing here?'

He crosses his arms and smirks—the same sassy attitude I remember from when we were kids. "They were my parents, too, you know. Not like I'd expect you to remember that."

I roll my eyes. "I mean what are you doing creeping around here dropping pans in the dark?"

Max heaves a box of cooking utensils onto the granite counter. "They cut the power, duh. No one to pay it. I'm just here sorting through some things I want to keep before the estate sale."

I squint at him and wonder if he's similarly sizing me up in the semi-darkness. It's been years since we've seen each other. He's more muscular than I remember, and his red hair is starting to thin at the front.

"Didn't Mom and Dad keep a generator somewhere around here?"

Max shrugs. "I dunno. The flashlights work fine for me."

Typical. Max was just like my parents that way: always taking the path of least resistance. Which is why we'd now have to split up all their assets with no direction from them.

"So," I say, leaning against the wall to feign nonchalance. "I suppose they never talked to you about a will?"

Max gives a dry chuckle. "Mom and Dad? No way. You know how they were. They said we could work it out." He pauses here and glances up at me slyly. "If you ever even came back," he adds. "But I'm not surprised, with that much money on the line."

I snort. "From the guy trying to swoop in and take what you want without even telling me! At least I texted you to let you know I was coming."

"Sorry, I think I blocked your number after all this time."

I'm fuming. The only person who came close to pushing my buttons this well was my ex-husband, but he wasn't nearly as good at it as my little brother.

"Let's try to be amicable here," I growl, drawing on all my New York professionalism. "We'll pack everything up, sell as soon as possible, and split the profits."

"Great," says Max cooly.

"Truce?" I ask, holding out my hand for him to shake. Max looks at my hand without taking it and looks back up at me.

"Sure . . . for now."

Max

Megan looks older than I remember. But that makes sense, because it's been seven years. Seven years since the last Christmas we spent together as a family. Seven years since she stormed out of the house and cut off all contact.

I expected her to look older, but I didn't expect her to look so sad. I'd heard from a cousin in Jersey that her marriage had ended, but I didn't know the details. Is that why she looked sad? Or was it something else? Regardless, she's the last person I wanted to see this holiday season. Growing up, we weren't close, which should come as a surprise to no one. A ten-year age gap will do that. By the time I came along, Megan was well-established as an only child, and she let me know, in no uncertain terms, that she wasn't happy to share her life with a new baby brother. Mom would laugh, remembering how Megan sulked in the corner on my first birthday. It seems that was the day she finally had to admit I was here to stay.

I sigh as I stare at the ceiling of my childhood bedroom. The glow-in-the-dark stars I put up there with my dad are still glimmering, faintly. I really miss him. I miss both my parents. But I'm also tired of crying. It's been awful trying to navigate everything alone: the hospital for Mom, both funerals, all the paperwork. The ironic thing is that I'm terrible at that stuff and Megan would have been way better at it—if she had any sort of empathy chip in her robot body.

My phone rings and I look down at the number. Ugh, Jason. My ex. Calling me at three a.m. Again. I squeeze the side button to decline the call, but even as I do, I worry about how I'm going to pay the rent next month. Jason is a mess, but he's a mess with platinum credit cards, and each time I decline one of his calls, he has more reason to stop helping me out while I look for a new place.

I throw the phone on the ground and roll over onto my side, hugging myself tight. It's no use. I get out of bed and tiptoe down the hall. I remember Megan to be a light sleeper, and now more than ever I don't want to wake her. I reach the familiar door at the end of the hallway and slowly turn the knob, careful not to let the hinges creak as I open it. I use my phone flashlight to illuminate the way up the stairs. As a kid, I knew the way by feel and could easily navigate in the dark, but it's been a long time since I've done this.

At the top of the stairs, I push open the door into my childhood sanctuary: the attic. The worn throw rug in the middle of the room is just the same, the little reading light and the cozy rocking chair. I can even see the moon and stars outside the big window. I feel a little shiver of delight run up my back. Everything is the same as I remember in my little library.

I crouch down to one of the shelves and run my fingers lovingly along the spines of my favorite books: *Robinson Crusoe*, *The Swiss Family Robinson*, *Treasure Island*, all the Harry Potters and Tolkien. I sigh and open one up to read by the moonlight, curling up on the little rocking chair. It's much too small now, and I move to the carpet. It happens so fast that I hardly even feel my eyes getting heavy, and before I know it, I've fallen fast asleep.

Megan

The next morning, I head from my room to the kitchen. On the way, I notice the door to Mom's studio is slightly open. I pull it closed without looking inside, as if doing so can also close the door to my memories of it.

Once I'm in the kitchen, I rummage through the stack of bills by the old landline till I find the most recent one from the electric company. A quick call, recitation of my credit card number, and verification that we have a smart meter is met with the promise that the power will be restored the same day, which surprises me, but I'll take it. After a quick trip to the store for essentials like milk, eggs, butter, and coffee, I return to the house to find a true Christmas miracle: the lights work! And I'm making pancakes in no time.

Not long after, Max walks in, completely disheveled. His auburn curls are frizzy and his shirt is rumpled.

"Morning," I say, raising an eyebrow. "It's almost nine o'clock."

Max rolls his eyes. "And?"

"Nothing," I say mildly, sliding a few pancakes onto the plate next to the stove. "Are you still bartending these days? I think I saw something on Instagram a while back."

"No," says Max, pulling out a pot. He fills it with water and then starts rummaging through drawers. "How'd you get the stove going? Did you find one of the lighters?"

"Power's back on," I tell him, waiting for a thank-you that doesn't come.

Instead, Max glances over at my bowl of batter. "Those are overmixed. Makes them come out all tough and chewy instead of light and fluffy."

I purse my lips. "They're fine," I say tightly. "Robert always liked them this way."

Max laughs. "Maybe that's why he left. 'Cause you forced him to eat chewy pancakes."

I stare at my brother. "What makes you so sure he left me, and it wasn't the other way around?"

"Just a guess," says Max with a shrug, grabbing some of my eggs out of the fridge and making room for himself at the stove.

"Mm," I say, dumping the rest of my overmixed batter down the sink. "Why don't we talk about your love life instead?"

"I'm single, too."

"And where are you living these days?"

"With a . . . friend."

"I see."

I sit down at the breakfast table and start eating my pancakes. I never even noticed before that they were chewy, but now that he's pointed it out, it's all I can feel in my mouth.

"I thought you were supposed to get all the lumps out when you mix the batter," I say, now thoroughly annoyed about this whole pancake situation.

Max shakes his head and joins me at the table with a glass of juice. Another thing I'd bought. "Common misconception. You want the dry ingredients just moistened. The lumps don't really matter."

I sip my coffee, and the silence that follows is deafening.

"Aren't you going to apologize?" Max asks finally.

I narrow my eyes. "Apologize for what?"

Max sets his glass down hard. It's odd seeing him like a real grown-up. In my mind, he feels permanently trapped at thirteen years old.

"Where do I start? For abandoning us, for leaving me to deal with Mom and Dad, for not being here when they died."

"I didn't abandon you. I just moved to New York. I was twenty-three, and I was ready to leave! It was nothing personal."

Max snorts. "Nothing personal, of course. What are we, business colleagues? How can you say I'm not personal when I'm your family? Mom and Dad might not have been the perfect parents, but you shouldn't have left like you did. You cut us out of your life completely."

I shake my head. I can feel tears welling up in my eyes. Even though I'd been desperate to leave, it was the hardest thing I'd ever done.

"I didn't come here to be lectured by my baby brother," I say quietly, getting up from the table. "Let's just box up this house and be done with it."

"Great, yes," I hear Max say as I walk back down the hall to my room. "Run away like you always do, Megan."

Megan

We spend the rest of the day boxing things up in separate rooms. I leave Max to finish up the kitchen while I start on my parents' bedroom. Although they eventually squandered it all, my parents had a lot of money at one point, and Mom's closet serves as proof of that. Anna Sui, Isabel Marant, Paul Poiret—she had style. As I sort bags and shoes into trash, Goodwill, and resell, I catch a whiff of perfume from one of her Hermès scarves, and I'm instantly transported back to my early adolescence.

I was in this room, a skinny, flat-chested teenager, looking at myself in the mirror. I was holding up a black and gold–beaded Bob Mackie dress, swaying back and forth, when Mom walked in. Surprised, and afraid she'd be mad at me for touching her things, I quickly threw it on the bed, but Mom just laughed.

"Oh honey," she chuckled. "You'll never have the body to pull that off."

Now, I narrow my eyes and sort through the dresses with determination. Even as I do, I can see that the largest ones are size 6. I've quickly grown to be an 8 or 10 after my divorce, but I'm determined to find that Bob Mackie dress and see if it will fit. When I finally find it at the back of the closet, it's a size 4, and I know without trying it on that it's way too small. It's just as beautiful as ever, and just as out of reach. I grit my teeth and lay it gently in the resell pile. Guess Mom was right after all.

I sort a few more pieces, but my heart isn't in it. I need a break, so I pad lightly out into the hallway.

"Max?" I call out. But everything is quiet. I think about making myself a peanut butter sandwich, but I'm not hungry. What I really want is a place I feel comfortable. One that isn't haunted by memories of an indifferent father and an impossible-to-please mother.

I walk to a door at the end of the hallway that I haven't opened in years. I stopped using the attic when I was thirteen or fourteen. I got busy with friends and thought it wasn't cool anymore. But now, something inside me craves it.

I quietly make my way to the top of the stairs and push open the door. "Max?"

He's lying on his back reading *Gulliver's Travels*, his feet up on the little rocking chair.

"Agh!" he yells, practically throwing the book across the room. "Stop creeping around like a weird ghost!"

"What are you doing in my attic?"

Max rolls onto his stomach to face me. "I'm sorry, *your* attic?"

"Yes!" I insist, gesturing around. "Mom and Dad let me put all this stuff up here when I was in second grade. It was *my* secret library."

Max puts his book down and sits up. He opens his mouth, then closes it. He looks legitimately stunned and a little hurt. "I thought it was my secret space."

I cross my arms, and even though I'm mad, I can't help but smirk. "Who did you think put all this stuff here?"

"I thought Mom and Dad made it for me," Max mutters, picking at the throw rug. "I always came up here when they fought."

"Me too," I say, sitting down next to him. "It's a lot quieter up here."

"Exactly."

We both sit in uncomfortable silence for a minute, and then I can't help myself.

"I cried every night for my first six months in New York, but I was too proud to come back, and too proud to admit how hard it was."

Max looks up at me. "Really? I had no idea."

I nod, trying not to get choked up. "When I was finally ready to come back, it seemed like you didn't even want me anymore."

Max shakes his head. "We always wanted you, Megan. Well . . . at least I did."

I look at the floor. I can't look at him. "I let all my issues with Mom and Dad come between you and me. You were always so much more like them than I was."

Max snorts. "You know better than anyone that's not such a good thing. I'll never forget what they wrote on my last assessment at culinary school, before I dropped out: 'A lot of creative potential but no follow-through.'" He pauses for a minute, then sighs. "I'm having a hard time with money. I've been bouncing between gigs, living off my ex. When I was little, I swore I'd never be like Mom and Dad, living the high life from job to job. But here I am."

I shrug. "They were creative geniuses. According to *Rolling Stone*, anyway."

"Oh, screw *Rolling Stone*!"

I start laughing, and then Max joins in, and suddenly we both can't stop. We're laughing till tears come down our cheeks.

"They might have been creative geniuses, but they sucked as parents."

"Agree," I say. "Hey, I think that's the first thing we've ever agreed on!"

Max smiles. "Maybe, yeah. At least in a really long time."

There's another long silence, but this one isn't so uncomfortable.

"Do you want to start over?" I ask.

He smiles and nods, and I hug my little brother for the first time in a very long time.

Max

The next morning is quiet. I shuffle out of bed and down the hall, and I notice that I feel a bit lighter. I'm not dreading seeing my sister.

This morning I'm the one who's up early, so I do a little grocery shopping of my own. I should have thanked her yesterday for getting food and paying to turn the power back on, but I wasn't in the mood.

Today, as I start to make my coffee, I set out an extra mug for Megan. It's a small gesture, but I certainly wouldn't have done it before.

I frown and look at the date on my phone. December 24. I hadn't counted on decorating, but now that we're here . . . I smile to myself. Why not?

I go to the hall closet and pull down a box labeled XMAS DECOR – DON'T TOUCH in Dad's handwriting. Mom had painted a little sleigh and reindeer next to it. She was always adding beautiful little sketches to the most mundane things—something I hadn't even noticed when she was still alive.

I heave the box down gently, and a decorative pinecone slips out the top and bounces across the floor.

"Hey, I remember these."

I set down the box and turn to find Megan, still sleepy-eyed and rumple-haired. She's picked up the pinecone and is smiling as she looks at it.

"Mom used to put these all around the candles as part of her tablescapes. I remember one year she even added pampas grass."

"Yeah," I say, opening the box and pulling out a tangled ball of lights. "That was the year the whole thing caught on fire."

Megan snort-laughs. "Yes!" she said. "It was the year I first invited a boyfriend over and I just about died of embarrassment."

She kneels next to me and gestures toward the lights. "Some things never change, huh?"

"What do you mean?" I ask, digging through the wad to find the plug.

"Well, why not coil them up neatly so the next person to open them doesn't have to deal with this mess?"

I laugh. "Megan, have you met our family? That's just not how we roll."

She sighs. "I know." But she doesn't sound as bitter about it as she used to. "I guess I don't mind being the one to straighten things out."

She gets to work pulling out knots in the cord while I plug them in. Half of them light up, with a few dimly fluttering, and a red one blinking erratically like a distress signal.

Over the next hour, I take out the lights that aren't working and set up the old tree, while Megan runs to Home Depot to get replacement bulbs. While she's gone, I make us breakfast: fluffy pancakes with syrup and boysenberry jam.

"Should we sit down?" I ask once she's back, but Megan shakes her head and picks up her plate. "Let's eat while we work," she suggests. "We've got a lot to do."

I roll my eyes. This would typically be enough to start a fight. But today, I'm deciding to let it ride.

I pick up my plate and join her outside. We find a cobwebby ladder on the side yard, and she holds the now-untangled coil of lights while I make my way along the eaves. I find Dad's nails that he used year after year, and hooking the strand of lights on each one makes me feel more connected to him than I have since he died.

Megan

I hadn't realized that taking things out of boxes is more fun than putting them in. The house is starting to feel alive again, rather than just a depressing chore of loose ends to tie up. After the lights, we move swiftly to the tacky lawn decorations.

"I always hated these," I say, pulling an inflatable Santa out from the garage. The Santa is in his swim trunks, sitting on a lawn chair under a coconut tree. "But now I think they're kinda cute."

Max just laughs. "Maybe your taste is evolving as you mature."

"You calling me old?" I say, cocking an eyebrow at him.

"Exactly," he says while hauling out a snowman dressed in an eighties jazzercise outfit. "Mom could never stand these, anyway. It was just Dad who thought they were hilarious."

"Yeah," I say wistfully. "I always thought Mom was so cool and sophisticated. But now I wonder if she couldn't take a joke."

"No need to wonder, Megs. She couldn't take a joke."

I look at my brother holding a five-foot-tall inflatable chicken with a Santa hat and scarf, and suddenly I can't stop giggling.

Max's eyes widen, and then he laughs along with me. "I'll have you know this is very serious Christmas decorating we're doing!" he announces, stabbing the air with his finger like he's making a proclamation. "Now, should we put them all in a group together, or space them out across the yard?"

We decide to put the Richard Simmons snowman with Vacation Santa, and the chicken with a flock of caroling flamingos. The chicken looks like a festive Godzilla among the flamingos, but we agree the birds belong together. We're just closing up the garage when I hear Max call out.

"Hey, remember this?"

I come around to the garage, where Max has pulled out our old tandem kayak. My stomach flip-flops.

"Let's go back inside," I suggest.

"No, wait. I remember you used to love going out on the kayak with Mom. You had that old-school camera that must have weighed twenty pounds."

"Yeah," I mutter. "I liked to take pictures of the neighborhood. I thought maybe I could be a photographer or something."

"I never knew that. What if we take it for a spin? For old time's sake."

I shake my head. "I'm tired," I lie. "I just want to go back inside."

I can see the hurt and surprise in his eyes. "Okay . . ." he says, pushing the kayak back into the garage and closing the door.

Inside, we put up the tree and keep pulling old decorations out of boxes, but the jolly mood has dissipated. Our conversation dribbles, and eventually runs out, even as we're still side by side. All I want is to be by myself. I take my opportunity when Max has his back to me, pinning up our old stockings at the fireplace.

I slip into the hallway and find Mom's old studio, the room I've carefully avoided since coming home.

Everything is just like I remember: easel and old paintbrushes in the middle of the room, the sink clogged with acrylic paint, the big window lighting up dust motes floating to the floor.

I head to the corner of the room, where Mom let me keep my pictures.

"Megan."

I hear my brother's voice from the doorway, and I turn around to see him standing there with his arms crossed. Again, I'm struck by how grown-up he looks—more like Dad than my little brother.

"I'm not going to let you run away again."

My cheeks flush red, but I let him come in. I don't make some nasty remark or storm out. I know he's right: I can't keep running away.

"I wanted to be an artist like Mom," I blurt out.

Max blinks, surprised. "But, I . . . is this like the library? I never saw you painting."

I open a drawer and pull out stacks of old photographs I'd taken over the years. Some were portraits of various family members and friends, but most were landscapes. My favorites were of the canals: the small, arched footbridges, a mother duck and her ducklings gliding across the water, an ivy-covered cottage with a jasmine trellis.

"Wow, Megs," Max says, sorting through the pictures. "These are really good."

"Thanks," I say flatly. I take a deep breath in. "This is the real reason I left on that Christmas seven years ago."

I pull out the last piece from the bottom of the drawer: not a photograph, but an 8 by 10–inch oil painting of the canals at Christmas in the gathering dusk. There's a red canoe in the foreground, a footbridge and houses strung up with lights in the middle. Palm trees frame the background, with the still water reflecting everything like a mirror.

As I hold it, the memory comes rushing back to me. I'd worked on the painting for months, basing it on one of my photographs from the year before.

Since Mom was a painter, I had always stuck to photography—that was at least slightly different to her work, and I loved taking pictures. But as a kid I'd gotten the itch for painting, and after many years, I'd finally been bold enough to attempt a piece like this.

I'd called my mom into the studio early on that Christmas morning and pulled it out of the drawer with a flourish.

"Ta da! It's a present for you," I'd said proudly.

I'll never forget the look on her face as she took it in: pure indifference. Her expert eye scanned it over, and then she set it down with a weak smile.

"Lovely, Megan. Thank you."

It felt like someone had popped a balloon in my chest, but I kept my smile. "I'm thinking of pursuing art more seriously," I admitted.

Mom cocked her head to the side. "As a hobby?"

"No, professionally."

"Hmm," Mom said, setting the picture down. She went to the sink and started running the faucet over some brushes, intentionally avoiding eye contact with me. "Not sure that's a good idea, hon," she continued over her shoulder. "It's very difficult to make it in the art world. You need a lot of talent."

I took this in silently, and maybe Mom noticed I wasn't saying anything, because she abruptly turned the water off and spun around. "Not that you aren't talented," she added quickly. "But it's just not for everyone."

And for whatever reason, that was it for me. I was done trying to please my mom, done living in her shadow, done dealing with my parents' financial highs and lows, their parties that trashed the house, their fights, all of it.

And Max had been the collateral damage.

I can barely look at him now, I'm so ashamed, but I force myself to. "I packed my bags and used all my savings to get a ticket to New York that night," I say, trying to keep my voice steady. "I got a job as an executive assistant at a big law office, met Robert, and, well, you know the rest."

Max doesn't say anything. He pulls me into a bear hug and lets me cry. When I'm done, he says, "Let's make you some tea."

Max takes my painting, and we go back out to the living room. I sit there, a little numb, still not ready to get back to decorating. He disappears into the kitchen to boil some water, and then I hear the opening chords of Brenda Lee's "Rockin' Around the Christmas Tree" coming over the speaker system.

Max comes back out, my painting in his hand, and I can see that he's found a frame for it. He gets a chair and takes down Mom's self-portrait from over the mantelpiece and puts up my little oil painting in its place. It looks ridiculous, so small in that big space, and I can't help but laugh. He grabs some gold tinsel and tacks it around the frame to fill it out a bit, and I help him. In the end, it looks like a kindergartener's project, but I love it.

Max

That night, we eat dinner in the living room. It's more comfortable on the couch than at the dining room table. As we enjoy our meal by the Christmas tree, I have to admit: my sister's painting is beautiful. Yes, it's amateur. Years of hearing art critiques from my parents has ensured that I'll notice areas with overworked brushstrokes and too much white paint. But all in all, it's not bad. She has an eye. I'm just mad I missed all those years with her over an oil painting.

"Max, this pork tenderloin is incredible," Megan says, breaking my thoughts. "How'd you get it so tender?"

I shrug. "It's all in the heat. And the balsamic glaze."

"And the goat cheese mashed potatoes? Perfection. You should start your own restaurant."

I clear my throat. Can I really admit this, out loud? I haven't even said it to myself. "I'd like to," I hear myself say.

Megan splutters a little. "Really? That's fantastic."

I feel my cheeks flush. "It's hard to start a restaurant. Expensive. And I don't exactly have a stellar résumé. I've mostly been bartending since I dropped out of school."

"Maybe I could help you."

It's the last thing I expect my sister to say, and I'm so caught off guard I don't know how to respond.

"I'm really organized," Megan continues hurriedly. "I could help with all the logistics. The business plan, securing funding."

"What about selling the house and going back to New York?"

Megan sets down her plate and looks at me squarely. "I've been thinking about that a lot. I think you should have the house."

I shake my head. "No, absolutely not. What about New York? How will you afford to live there on your own?"

Megan sighs. "Now that I'm finally home, I'm not sure I want to go back. To be honest, I don't have much to go back to."

We both let this sink in, the weight of it.

"Maybe we can help each other," I suggest. "What if we share the house and live here together, at least for now? We'll cancel the estate sale."

Megan looks up, surprised. "You want that?"

I nod. "It can be the fresh start we both need."

Megan sips her tea and glances toward Mom's studio. "I'm not sure. There's just a lot of memories here. You know, good and bad."

"Why don't you make Mom's old studio your office? Just because it was their house doesn't mean we can't make it our own."

Megan smiles. "I guess that's true. And I'll need a place to work if I'm managing things for the restaurant."

I start looking around the room. "I've never loved the avant garde vibes," I announce, gesturing to the teal walls. Megan glances at one of the many sculptures in the room—a Rubenesque Sphinx with the body of a chubby lady, a tail, wings, and clawed feet.

"That one in particular has always freaked me out," Megan mutters. She pauses. "I never felt like I could question what's in here. But why not? I love the idea of making it our own."

"Maybe something cozier," I muse, prodding at an abstract throw pillow made from rainbow-colored lint balls. "Less of a Rubik's cube for your eyes, and more of a relaxing crossword."

"As long as we keep the yellow door," Megan says. "I never liked it, but it makes this house our home. Our street wouldn't be the same without it."

"Deal," I agree.

She holds up her empty tea mug. "To finally running toward something, and not away."

"Oh, I'll definitely cheers to that."

We clink our mugs, and I can hear the faint sound of carolers from somewhere across the canals. Outside, lights ripple on the water.

"Still wanna take the kayak out?" Megan asks, practically reading my mind.

Minutes later, we're out on the water, gliding through the soft glow of yellow, green, and red shimmering on the surface. Neither of us says much, but for the first time in years, the silence feels peaceful, and that's one of the best Christmas presents I've ever had.

About the Author

Katherine Rea is a writer from Saratoga, California. She currently lives on California's Central Coast with her husband, two children, and an orange cat. When she's not writing, she enjoys reading, spending time outside, and traveling.

You can find Katherine on Instagram: @katherine_rea_writes

To learn more about Katherine, visit her website at: katherinerea.com

A Holiday Homecoming

A Holiday Homecoming

Laura Turner

Chapter One

NATHAN, December 3, 2025, Kuwait, 0600 Hours

I cinch closed my duffel bag carry-on. I've been living in this bunker for a year. It was hot and humid, so I don't have much clothing other than my uniforms.

"See you down the road, partner," my roomie Michael says, hugging me. Tapping me on the back.

In many ways, I can't believe I'd agreed to come at all. To Kuwait of all places. I'd been offered a desk job at Fort Drum for the same, even slightly better, pay. And since the US had bombed Iran in an impromptu, albeit against the United Nations code, attack, I had no idea I'd feel like such a sitting duck.

But I knew I could retire at the end of the tour. And that time has come. If I'd taken the desk job, I would have to work another year or more. And the guys . . . I couldn't let down my guys.

I cannot let them down.

"We love you, Santos," the group of them gathered around me in the common area, each embracing me briefly.

"We will definitely see you on the other side. Get out of here while you can," my buddy Kenneth says.

For Christine. I love you beyond reason.

I hate to leave them behind. At the same time, I *so* can't wait to get home to the States.

To my family.

I've done several tours including Afghanistan and Desert Storm, so I've seen some things. But this one was by far the hardest. I had to say a final goodbye to one of my brethren, Kendrick. Send him home to his family for the holidays in a pine box after his tank drove over a landmine.

Yes, I will be retiring now. But I will never, ever forget.

I think of Kendrick as I step up onto the helipad, the chopper blades whirring overhead.

I throw my bags in before me and climb in. Put on my head gear, and the chopper lifts off in a New York minute.

LAURIE, November 5, 2025, New York, 10:15 a.m.

I lace up my sneakers for my morning run. I've already mowed the lawn, fed the pups, and called the plumber about the leaking hot water heater. I need a bit of me time.

Right now, I just need to stay busy. Hope and pray Nathan makes it home in one piece. I have done everything I can think of during the last year to keep myself occupied: worked extra hours stocking shelves at the Lakeville Grocery, tried to fill my time with weekly visits with my friends from high school.

"We've got you," they all said.

I am strong. I am as strong as I can be on the outside. Nathan needs me to be. But on the inside, my anxiety is always threatening to blow up on me.

I have gone to the protests with my handmade signs that say, "Free Press."

And I've watched the news and rallies around the country on TikTok.

But when the United States bombed Iran and the retaliation messages came across social media as, "We're coming for your troops to put them in body bags," it was more than I could handle.

I give my sneakers one last tug and secure the pups. I need to go out alone for this one, as advertised.

Christmas.

He will be home for the holiday.

Or so I hope.

I step out onto the street, the pavement cold beneath my feet, and I put one foot in front of the next. I inhale the chilly air. Winter is here in our small upstate town.

Thank God for this small town, I think to myself. The supportive community. My mother.

I take off down the road and pick up speed once I hit the trail marker.

LAURIE, December 5, 2025, New York, 5:45 p.m.

"You ladies good to walk?"

They both nod. I open the hatch to the back of the SUV and pull out the handmade sign.

Irene, Nathan's younger sister, is in charge of the leis. And Malinka, Nathan's older sister, the boom box.

We all gather our wares and head to the lobby of the airport.

"Hey, Marybeth, it's awesome to see you," I say to the wife of a fellow military compatriot, his family gathered about. The local gang is all represented. All except Kendrick's family.

I tamp down on my sadness, my anxiety. But the reality remains. No, Kendrick will not be getting off that plane.

And then I think back to my days in college. My studies to become a teacher. My husband's loyalties. And a quote comes into my mind. It's by John Donne: "No man is an island, entire from itself; every man is a piece of the continent, a part of the main...any man's death diminishes me, because I am involved in mankind and therefore never send to know for whom the bell tolls; it tolls for thee."[1]

The ladies and I set up our wares at the gate in a small corner of the airport lobby below the escalator. I inhale, peering up at the moving screen. Flight 62 has arrived. And if all my hopes and prayers are answered, Nathan will be on it.

LAURIE, December 5, 2025, Home Base, 11:32 p.m.

We lay in bed that night. I am on my side, and he is on the other.

"What are you thinking?" I say.

---

[1] From *Devotions upon Emergent Occasions*, Meditation 17; John Donne, *The Norton Anthology of English Literature*, Sixth Edition. Copyright 1990 by W.W. Norton & Company.

"You know," is his reply.

His lips moved from a hyphen to a slight U-shape when he stepped off the plane. But they quickly returned to a hyphen once more in no time.

I am not sure what to say in this moment.

How can I comfort my husband?

"Do you want to talk about it?" I ask. "Would that help?"

He says nothing, and I watch on as he lay on his back next to me, pinching his eyes closed. I watch his chest rise and fall.

Rising and falling.

We dreamt of this moment. When he returned home from his final tour. When we could make love to each other and know the nightmare was over.

I gently place my hand on his shoulder. Trace it along his arm. The tattoos he's collected from his tours.

"I love you, you know. More than anything. I will not let this break us," I say. But in this moment, I don't know.

He continues to lie there next to me, motionless. His eyes remain squeezed shut. I remove my hand from his arm when he shifts slightly.

He then reaches over the bedside, lifts up a glass of water.

He takes a drink, sets it back.

I am hopeful, perhaps he will say something. Comfort me now. Make me feel like it is all going to be all right.

But he turns from me then, reaches up, and clicks off the light telescoping our bed. He turns to his side away from me.

"Goodnight, babe," I say under my breath. "Welcome home, sweetheart."

Chapter Two

NATHAN, November 30, 1986, Burger King, New York, 3:32 p.m.

I am happy to have a job. Never mind that it's flipping burgers at the local fast-food joint. I am happy to have income.

Some of my family has recently immigrated to the area from the Philippines. We are all simply trying to blend in.

"I need a burger. Fries. Milkshake," Laurie announces.

Okay, so the manager is not bad to look at either.

I feel a smile play at my lips. "Coming up!"

I'd learned to speak English the way a lot of Filipinos do, by listening to American music. Learning the lyrics.

I love Sunday dinners with my family for this reason. Sometimes we have pig roasts in the backyard. Then we fire up the Karaoke machine.

I flip the burger. "Hot off the grill," I say. Our eyes meet. They are the brightest blue. And her hair, curly and dark. I can tell even with it pulled back into a net. Also, to be honest, I saw her the other day with her flowing locks outside the required bun.

Her gaze holds mine for a moment. Probably a bit longer than the order requires. If only she would give me a chance. I've never really believed in love at first sight, but I think I'm starting to.

I find myself whistling while I cook the next round.

I know what I have to do. I need to show her that I'm getting my footing here in the United States. *But how can I show her that I am more than a cook at a fast-food restaurant?* There must be a way I can slip in that I've enlisted. And beyond that, I'm also a mechanic.

When I leave work that evening, I find her under the hood of her car in the parking lot.

"Damn thing won't start," she says of the old compact five-speed she's driving.

"Let's see what we can do about that," I say.

LAURIE, November 30, 1986, Burger King, New York, 5:15 p.m.

I'll be honest: After my parents' divorce, I was never interested in long-term relationships. It actually kind of fucked me up wholesale.

I won't go into details about them.

I had highest honors in high school, took advanced placement classes even. I hoped to be a teacher. But once I enrolled in college and moved in, the sorority kind of took over.

My grades plummeted. I dropped out in my final semester.

I did keep my managerial position at the local fast-food restaurant, though. Still, *was this as far as life would take me?* I wondered.

"Can I help you? No. Let me help you," Nathan Santos says the day my car stops running.

It's the dead of winter, an oppressively cold day in Upstate New York. There I am, cursing my past mistakes, nursing my regret. And he swoops in like a knight in shining armor. Well, he *was* wearing a cook's cape. A chef's apron.

He covers me in his coat. His dark eyes are kind. "Come on. Let me, will you?"

He leans in and opens the pan to my engine compartment. He opens the choke, tells me to gas it, and the car sputters to a start.

I gaze at him. "Thank you," I say, and I notice his hair is short, neatly trimmed in a military style. His tanned skin goes taught at the corners of his mouth when he smiles in a severely adorable way.

"Ma'am," he says and begins to walk away.

"Wait," I say and run to him. I kiss him on the cheek.

"I've signed for the Army. They are deploying me to North Carolina for basic," he says. "But I'd like to see you before I leave."

We exchange numbers.

A smile tugs at my lips as I drive out of the parking lot of the local fast-food restaurant.

NATHAN, December 24, 2025, Upstate New York, 0900 Hours

Today I have to do the unthinkable. I must go to visit the family of my fallen compatriot. It is wintertime in New York, and the holiday is falling in.

I knock carefully on the door.

"Oh," Kendricks's wife says when she opens. And then she immediately gathers me in, embracing me in a warm hug.

Her home is beautifully decorated.

"I am so sorry. I don't have the right words to say to you," I say.

"You need not say anything more," she says.

She walks to the kitchen and brings back two cups of tea. "The kids are with their grandparents," she says.

"I'm having a hard time," I say honestly.

"Nathan, you have to know how much Kendrick thought of you. He would want you to go on in his honor," she says.

Her eyes are bright blue I noticed, much like my own wife's.

"What about you?" I ask.

"Nathan, Kendrick did what he felt called to do. This is the sacrifice we must make for the calling."

"I keep wondering why it wasn't me," I say.

And then I begin to cry. Literally cry. The tears come. I do not mean for this to happen.

"Go, live your life. Love your family, embrace them for all you're worth," she says.

She gathers me in then in a tight hug. I do not have any words for her. The right words do not come to me. I think of my wife then, Laurie. How I have been so cold. But these feelings . . . Loss. Regret.

Guilt.

"Join us for Christmas dinner," I say.

NATHAN, December 24, 2025, Home Base, 11:32 a.m.

I return home from Kendrick's homestead and the smells of Christmas dinner are wafting from the kitchen.

"The children were planning to come home this afternoon," Laurie says.

There is a pig roast on the table. Our home is beautifully decorated. While I was away, Laurie had the house remodeled. The living room is now a bright shade of yellow. Bright. Like her. *She is the woman I love.*

I want to say this then, but I still do not have the right words. I know this sounds impossible. But the guilt, it continues to ravage me.

Laurie pulled the pig from the backyard pit herself. She is preparing it exactly the way I like. Perfect spices. Perfect complements.

"I need you to move the cars out of the garage," she says as if I have been here all along, as if I'd never left. *Like we're normal people.*

We were told by the social workers about the new normal. What could happen with the PTSD.

"Of course," I say.

I pause to watch her wandering about the kitchen, reaching for things she needs in the refrigerator, the cupboard, our cupboard. I begin to observe a warmth overcome me. *Do I always have to harden my heart?* I feel somewhat of a softness embrace me as I watch her in her apron. Like the one I used to wear when we met. *She is still so youthful.*

"I cleaned off the Karaoke machine," she says.

And I sense it. I feel a smile starting.

"That's wonderful," I say. And all at once, I think of the songs I wanted to sing when I had the chance again. All the songs I thought of in my head while deployed, those that kept me going.

That and . . .

I did not speak the thoughts I had in my mind. I knew I needed to show her. I do not want to waste one moment, one *more* moment. I turn her by the shoulders, take the items out from her hands, straighten her apron, and then I lean in and I kiss her for all I am worth.

Chapter Three

LAURIE, December 5, 2001, Home Base, 11:56 p.m.

It has become an impossible burden to bear, I think to myself. I think I will explode if Nathan is deployed one more time. The stolen phone calls. This crazy lifestyle.

NATHAN, July 25, 2002, Upstate New York, Civilian Quarters, 1730 Hours

I don't know why I am having dinner with this woman. Oh, yes I do. My wife has left me. "Yes, of course I'll have dinner with you. I'd love to. I've been waiting," Erica had said.

Erica is a coworker at the civilian job I have at the barracks. She gave me the side eye. Every day. But I am married.

At least I think I am.

Was.

Until I wasn't married anymore. Not really. Laurie. I lost her on the last deployment to Afghanistan. She said she couldn't take it anymore. The panic. The anxiety. The not knowing if I would come home in a body bag.

She loves spending time with her friends. "They are so light," she said, "so problem-free."

I try to understand. But it's hard. And I must respect her wishes. I am not like that. I am not going to keep her if she doesn't want to be kept.

So here I am out to dinner with Erica.

"More wine?" I ask.

And she nods. She is attractive. Brown, curly hair. Light amber eyes. Any man in their right mind would give their eye teeth to be out with this woman. And she clearly likes me.

We chat and she tells me of her relationship woes.

Divorce. Two children.

I care. But I don't. Erica is a warm body.

But Laurie . . .

I cannot force someone to love me.

To be clear, I am not trying to make Laurie jealous. I am merely trying to fill the empty space in my heart. Especially during the holidays.

This is the life I have chosen. Of service. To my country.

Sometimes that burden or honor or whatever it is is bigger than both of us.

I was totally transparent. But now I fear it is or has ruined us. And without Laurie, I don't have strength. *Laurie makes me strong.*

The check comes and Erica slides it across the table toward her. "I'll take that. This one's on me," she says with a wink. Pours me another glass of wine.

LAURIE, July 26, 2002, Upstate New York, Civilian Quarters, 10:31 a.m.

I stumble up the stairs to my husband's workplace.

I am about to make a crazy fool of myself, but I don't even care.

"Excuse me, Erica?" I say once I have been shown to her cubicle. And she turns.

"Could I have a word?"

She catches my gaze. Hair cascading to her shoulders. She may be ten years younger than me. It's so hard to tell these days.

"I understand we have a mutual, shall I say, admiration for someone," I say.

Hopefully this gets the ball rolling.

She scoffs. "We do?"

I don't blame her. I haven't exactly been the model supportive wife. *But who wouldn't crack under pressure?* Who wouldn't give up when they are constantly in an emotional vice-grip and can see no way out?

Thinking of the one they love disintegrating. Leaving for years at a time, or maybe never to be seen again.

Who wouldn't want peace from that?

And for what?

The choices are made by an *administration*. One that we hope has regard for individual lives.

It's more than a paycheck.

These are our lives.

"I need to speak to you alone," I tell her.

And she scoffs again.

Fine. Let her scoff. I am here on a mission of my own.

We enter a back office common room. I open the large wooden door and enter behind her. She wafts in, all perfume, short skirt, taupe business jacket to match.

"Have a seat," I say.

She does as I ask with a *make it quick I have things to do* face.

"I am here because I want my husband back," I say.

NATHAN, July 26, Upstate New York, Civilian Quarters, 6.15 p.m.

My WIFE has fought for me. She is stronger than any soldier, any mortal, any army.

LAURIE, December 25, 2025, Home Base, 3:06 p.m.

At noon, the guests begin to arrive. Nathan's youngest sister is the first through the door. She offers me her colorful Filipino salad, and I receive it gratefully.

"He's in the living room," I say.

"I don't know what to say to him," she offers. "I've tried everything."

She helps, holds open the oven as I pull the pig roast from warming.

"Challenge him to a karaoke duel," I say.

She laughs.

"It sounds so simple, doesn't it? But that always *was* his favorite part of the holiday and family gatherings. Always has been."

The family continues to arrive. We all spread out at the table, and the air is light with the festivities. I watch Nathan. He embraces each family member as they approach, welcome him home. The mood in the house turns over as loved ones continue to enter.

My mom and dad.

My brothers and their families. A few dogs.

Our own two grown children.

Nathan's older sister.

And soon Kendrick's wife, his two children.

The dinner continues to buzz with chats and hugs.

Soon, Irene picks up the karaoke microphone.

"Let's go," she says.

Nathan walks onto the platform. He cues up his song.

"This is for Kendrick. This also goes out to my second family and for all who have sacrificed. You are here with us on this holiday and forever in our hearts," he says. "This is a song that has been on my mind for some time. It's called, 'He Ain't Heavy. He's My Brother.'"

LAURIE, December 25, 2025, Home Base, 11:32 p.m.

That night in bed we both climbed in, each to our own sides. My husband has shed his robe, and I once more view his cacophony of tattoos.

He turns to face me. I roll up on my side, trace a peace symbol on his arm.

The children have come to stay briefly, secure in their old rooms. Our son and his wife are now expecting, they announced tonight.

"We are about to become grandparents," I say.

"I know," he returns.

"What will you wish to share with our newborn grandbaby?" I ask.

He lay on his back, smiling thoughtfully. "That there is goodness in this world. There is love. There is kindness. We must keep our guard up sometimes. But in the end, it's the love of family that makes it all worthwhile," he says.

"I love you, babe, you know?"

He turns to me then. He traces my face with his finger, my cheeks, my lips, my nose, painting me with his hand like he can't believe I'm real.

"I'm happy to be home," he says. A tear escapes his eye then. One lone tear.

And then I well up too. I try to press them back. But the tears come and I surrender, lean in.

He leans into me. Embraces me like he never wants to let me go.

I exhale and sink into his arms. And then all at once the whole entire world falls away.

And for that moment, it's just us.

About the Author

Laura Turner is an honorary graduate of Nazareth University's English Literature program. Her essays and short stories have been published most notably in Spillwords Press (feature and nomination for story of the month), Micromance Magazine, Eve Magazine, Conceit Magazine, and (editor's choice) in the Friday Flash Fiction literary journal. She has received nominations for BestMicrofiction 2025, the Edinburgh Literary Award, and longlisted for The Cupid Prize, Excellence in Love Literature. She is a former medical student and lives in Upstate New York.

You can find Laura on Instagram:
@lauraturnerauthor

To learn more about Laura, visit her website at:
https://lauraturnerwrites.com

Snowed Inn at Christmas

Snowed Inn at Christmas

Rick Ferguson

Chapter One

On Christmas Eve morning, Steven Caufield was an hour late for work. He'd texted Andrea, his administrative assistant, the night before, informing her he'd be skipping the company employee Christmas dinner that night. His reason was that he'd offered to take a client out for drinks—the man's flight was canceled because of severe weather at his destination. Steven would entertain the stranded businessman while delivering one more pitch for his services. That's what Steven Caufield did.

In the past five years, Steven had scaled the corporate ladder from account executive to creative director to the combined role of VP of sales and creative. He'd done this at the oldest advertising firm in Toronto—Green & Mackenzie.

When Steven entered the office that morning, he knew he looked hungover on top of the "tired" appearance he'd been carrying recently: his hair was showing signs of graying, and his typically energetic, almost athletic pace had been missing for weeks.

He struggled to remove his overcoat before heading down the hall. When Andrea asked if was ready for coffee, he shook his head, which caused her to pause in the breakroom to make him a cup while he kept walking.

Steven was staring at his desk when Andrea appeared with a steaming cup in one hand and two extra-strength Tylenol in the other.

"You're a magician," he said.

His headache sapped the energy he would need this morning, and he'd just remembered he had to inform Andrea of his Christmas plans so she could finish his out-of-office schedule.

"My plans are incomplete. I'm picking Wellesley up at school and dropping her off at April's parents' cottage by five o'clock, then heading to our cottage on the other side of the lake. I want to avoid the 'sit-down' with my in-laws where they give us 'the talk' tonight."

Andrea left him alone with his headache and sent him a reminder text.

"Don't keep Wellesley waiting at school—you know how 'simp' that looks. I canceled your 11:00 Zoom. It'll wait until the New Year. Don't dawdle on the way north. The Weather Network is reporting that the storm is moving north faster than expected!"

Chapter Two

Steven slowly entered the school driveway and cautiously approached the designated pickup spot. It was easy to spot his daughter, slouching against the wall with her backpack at her feet. She was not alone. He was glad to see her conversing with another student—it appeared she wasn't the last one to be picked up by their parents.

She glanced in his direction as he stopped the SUV, but once she recognized him, she returned her attention to the girl.

"The Death Stare," Steven commented. It was now his turn to wait.

As the snowflakes started falling, the passenger door opening caught his attention.

"Hi, sweetheart!" he greeted her as she struggled with the backpack, finally throwing it on the seat behind her.

"We have to go home and get some stuff. Mom just texted me," she reported.

Receiving the news from his daughter instead of his wife annoyed him. It was affirmation, he thought, that April was communicating with him indirectly through their daughter. Steven calculated that this detour would add at least half an hour to the drive north.

He made small talk with Wellesley by asking her how her day was, but he stopped asking when subjected to one-word responses. She quickly reached for her earbuds and began listening to music on her phone, clearly ready to ignore him.

Steven was now focused only on his driving and reached for the wiper control to clear the droplets of melting snowflakes accumulating on the windshield. The expected holiday traffic had begun but was building faster than usual, accelerated by the impending storm.

Steven hesitated to go inside when they reached the family home on Royal York Road. Wellesley exited the vehicle the second it stopped and quickly unlocked the front door. Steven hadn't been home since he'd moved out three weeks earlier. He finally exited the vehicle and went in, looking around to see if anything had changed. A large spruce tree stood prominently in the living room's bay window, completely adorned with the family decorations they had acquired over the years.

Walking toward the kitchen, he passed potted red and white poinsettias and other familiar and new decorations, tastefully creating the perfect seasonal atmosphere. He entered the kitchen and removed two water bottles from the fridge. He was about to close the door when he noticed a bottle of white wine chilling.

"Might come in handy for dinner," he told himself as he removed it.

Wellesley suddenly appeared in the doorway, dropping her suitcase beside her. "Mom wants you to bring the large roasting pan for tomorrow," she directed.

"When did she say that?"

"Now. She texted me."

Steven rolled his eyes and wondered how long this communication would continue. He searched the overhead cupboards for the pan, placed the wine bottle in it, and they left the house.

With the trip's destination on his vehicle's screen navigator, they drove north. The estimated arrival time was 3:45. He turned on the radio traffic report, which warned of a lengthy backup and lane closures on Highway 400, his intended route north. He quickly changed routes to go east toward Highway 115.

As they reached the entrance ramp to Highway 401, Steven slowed the SUV to a crawl. As the temperature slowly decreased, the snowfall increased and accumulated on the road. Streams of vehicles eventually slowed even further when the conga line of snowplows forced their way onto the road with almost military precision.

The trip display suddenly showed 4:15 as the new ETA.

Stop-and-go traffic had him mindlessly paying attention to the space between his SUV and the vehicle ahead, but this kind of driving required no thought. The monotony of the slow driving allowed him to reflect on his current predicament. His additional responsibilities as vice president of sales had taken a toll on his marriage over the last few years.

He thought back to a conversation with April in which she'd questioned him about his priority change. "There are four of us in our family now—your job is the recent addition. It's the one you want to spend the most time with," she'd accused.

"It's not like that," he'd defended.

"That's how *you* see it. We see a husband and father who doesn't have time for us. If you were having an affair, well, at least it would explain your absence."

"Don't be silly. You know I'm not having an affair."

Cheating on his wife, even if he were the type, would be almost impossible. His assistant Andrea knew every one of his moves inside and outside the office. And even though April made jokes about her being his "work wife," April and Andrea were close friends. Andrea always had her back.

The first week of December, he'd come home after eleven p.m. He had neglected to call too many times now to say he wouldn't be home for dinner. When he arrived home that night, April was waiting for an apology or an explanation, and he'd given neither.

That had been Steven's tipping point. His rationale tank was empty. He'd gone upstairs, and they spoke no more that evening. Before he went to bed, he'd packed a suitcase, and the next morning, before April was awake, he'd taken the first step in moving out.

April couldn't believe it at first. She tried calling a truce, suggesting they meet somewhere to talk privately, but he told her he needed some space and time to think.

He knew his refusal had shocked her. She accused him of no longer being interested in his role as a family man.

This drive to the cottage was gifting him something he had lacked for a long time—peace. Wellesley was content to text her friends and do whatever else pre-teens do when they are under the spell of their e-devices.

It occurred to Steven then that *he* was the one responsible for this. Sure, he could blame the company for demanding more of his time, but April was right about one thing—he was choosing business over family. He realized his family was worth more than whatever reward he got from the business. The conundrum was: how to make a new work-life balance work? He had no answer to that.

As they approached Oshawa, the cloud cover had insulated the ground from whatever sunlight remained as it descended on the horizon. It was 3:45 when he exited Highway 401 to make a rest stop and top up the gas tank.

"C'mon, girl, let's stretch our legs and get a treat at Tim Hortons," he said to Wellesley.

Back in the Cadillac, the trip navigator read 5:30 as the ETA. He'd have to call April soon to tell her they'd be late. He found the Highway 115 ride relatively easy. Turning off Highway 28, he was surprised to see the road recently plowed, and the wind calmed. The low-watt amount of sunlight that lingered was gone now, and the only lights other than headlights illuminating the drive came from dim, sparsely placed pole lights along the road.

When they reached the bend in the road curving close to the Otonabee River, the colored Christmas lights on some vacation homes lifted the gloominess.

Steven thought he saw blinking colored lights flashing between the trees as they approached Lakefield Old Bridge. At the entrance to the bridge, OPP cruisers, one facing north and one facing south, blocked the entrance. Officers placed flares on the road and waved flashlights outside their vehicles.

He rolled down his window to get an explanation. An officer approached Steven's SUV.

"Good evening, sir. The bridge is closed. We have a tractor-trailer blocking both lanes on the other side of the bridge."

"When do you think the bridge will be cleared?"

By now, the officer must've repeated this story ten times.

"We called for a tow truck when the accident happened about an hour ago. We're still waiting. It will take time to get the truck out when it shows up. The bumper was almost welded to the guardrail. You should find a spot to wait it out. Almost everything is closed now because . . ."

"It's Christmas Eve."

The officer wiped some snow from his face and asked, "Where are you heading?"

"Not far—just up to Clear Lake."

"Wow. You have two choices. Go back through Lakefield, that's probably your best bet. But, from what I hear, it's still snowing pretty heavily up there if you go north. I don't recommend that."

Steven didn't like that idea either. He didn't want to backtrack. One idea was to call April and suggest they stay at the family cottage tonight—he knew April wouldn't like that, especially if the bridge still wasn't open the next morning.

"If you go south, and cross at Lakefield, you'd probably want to take 25 along the lake up to Young's Point. I suggest you take Preston Road to the 12th Line. Preston is plowed. I came down it before I got here."

"Thanks, officer," Steven said as he carefully turned the SUV around and entered the coordinates on the trip navigator.

He didn't realize Wellesley had been paying attention to the conversation.

"How late are we going to be, Dad?"

The ETA had not reset, but he made his own estimate: "Five o'clock now. Allow for some driving to the conditions, maybe six at the latest. It's not too late, but we should call your mother."

Sure enough, the software agreed with him, though an additional problem was about to surface. He didn't know Preston Road that well and couldn't remember if it ended at the 12th Line. It did, but he was confusing Preston Road with Northey's Road. Just as they passed the Dixie Truck Centre, the trip navigator signal froze, as did the phone signal; his GPS was no longer working.

"Call your mom now!" he instructed his daughter.

The command in his voice unnerved Wellesley. "There's no service!" she told him.

The wind picked up, and visibility worsened. Steven had to keep the wipers going at increasing speeds as wet snowflakes clung to the windshield. The rapid change in the weather surprised him. He tried reading the road sign as he coasted to the stop sign ahead to avoid skidding through it. Snow completely caked the sign, making it illegible.

Steven guessed he was at Miller Road, so he turned right, expecting the road to connect with Highway 25. He could feel the vehicle's hesitation as they made their way east. The snow was past the tire wall, and his traction control system activated. It felt as if they were walking in deep snow and had to struggle to lift their feet out of it. The vehicle hesitated, and then he knew: the SUV was stuck.

He was about to scream obscenities when he realized he was with his daughter and somehow restrained himself.

"Where are we?" Wellesley asked, peering into the darkness.

Steven tried reversing the SUV, but the snow was too deep. He thought it may be possible to dig the vehicle free, but the way the wind whipped the surrounding snow, he knew it'd be a chore. He tried it briefly before realizing snow was coming at him almost as fast as he removed it. He climbed back into the car to take a break. He didn't want to let his daughter know how hopeless this was.

"Maybe we could go there and get help?" she asked as he caught his breath.

"What?" he asked as she pointed to the only distant light.

Ahead on the left was a light, two in fact, illuminating what looked like a doorway. The blankets of snow that hung in the wind like clean laundry obscured the rest of the structure.

"I didn't see that before," he said. "Do you think you can walk that far?"

Chapter Three

Steven was grateful for one thing—he and April hadn't raised an impuissant child.

"Put on my other winter jacket and pull the strings tight on the hood."

She gave him no argument, and the pair trudged through the drifts, keeping their heads down as they wound toward the lights. Steven gripped her hand tight, ensuring she wouldn't stray, but also helping keep her upright and preventing the drifts from swallowing her up.

Steven looked up once or twice to ensure they were headed for the lights. As they got closer, he saw the outline of a house. It was nearly invisible in the night—white clapboard with a snow-covered roof against a completely white backdrop. It appeared as if there were lights behind the drawn blinds, but he couldn't look up long enough to be sure.

"What do we do if no one is home?" Wellesley asked.

It hadn't occurred to Steven, but it should've: Would he break the law and a window if they had to?

"The lights are on, honey. Someone must be home. People in the country don't leave their lights on when they aren't home." He was reassuring *himself* of this theory more than her.

The driving wind was clinging to him like icy hands, testing the resistance of his down-filled parka. They finally reached a front porch. Someone had cleared the stairs, but drifts had formed around them. They climbed the few steps to the door and instinctively stomped their feet before the threshold.

Steven looked for a doorbell and instead saw a large heart-shaped brass knocker. He gave it several hard raps to announce their presence.

The snow-whitened pair stood on the welcome mat, shivering, but not for long. The door opened, and Steven and Wellesley were awash in warm light.

"Come in!" a voice said, and a sturdy but wrinkled pair of hands reached out to them, gently summoning them inside.

Steven tried his best to wipe the coating of snow from his coat and helped Wellesley do the same.

Before he knew it, someone had removed his coat and hat, and his daughter received the same help.

He faced a lady with long, silver hair parted in the middle as he adjusted to the warmth. Her rosy cheeks and soft eyes reminded him of someone's grandmother. Small, rounded-lens glasses were perched high on her small nose. A green and red festive shawl was draped around her shoulders. She quickly placed the shawl around Wellesley.

"We were wondering if you were coming in!" she announced.

Steven was taken by surprise. "You sound as if you were expecting us!"

"We weren't, but when we saw the headlights, I said, 'Now if someone's out driving this Christmas Eve, they may not get too far. Better put another log on the fire.'"

Steven looked past her, noticing the edge of a fireplace, and glimpsed the flickering flames.

"Come in, come in and warm yourselves. Let me introduce you to everyone."

At first, Steven had heard no sounds in the house, but now he heard laughter and music.

"I'm Julia Alt. Welcome to Hollidays' Inn!" she announced as she beckoned them to follow her down the hallway to a brightly decorated room.

The spectacle overwhelmed Steven and Wellesley. The white-paneled room was strung with fresh cedar garland around the perimeter of the high ceiling. In one corner of the room stood a large Scotch pine Christmas tree, lit with multicolored incandescent lights, traditional glass ornaments, multiple strings of popcorn and cranberries, and old-fashioned silver tinsel icicles. A golden-haired angel dressed in white, with a silver halo above its head, capped the tree.

His attention was drawn to the enormous red-brick fireplace, which rose from its stone hearth to almost two-thirds of the way up the wall. The firedog contained logs that appeared to be cut from telephone poles. Steven gravitated to its warmth, and the chill that'd taken over him on the journey from the car had left.

"My heavens, I've forgotten my manners," Julia said. "I haven't introduced you to everyone!"

She took Steven by the arm (he suddenly realized that Wellesley had both hands wrapped around the other) and led them to an older couple sitting on a loveseat. The pair stood up in unison as Julia acquainted them.

"This is Jean and Rob."

The man quickly shook Steven's hand as if they'd known each other for years.

"I'm Jean and she's Rob." He laughed.

His wife slapped him playfully on the shoulder and said, "He *always* does that. I'm Roberta. He calls me Rob. And he's Eugene, but he's never liked it, so we call him Gene."

Gene was still having fun with the joke. "Did you see the look?" he chuckled.

Before Steven could introduce himself, they were hurried toward a piano in the room's corner.

"And these are our newlyweds, Peter and Nicole," Julia announced.

Steven shook the hands offered to him, while Gene broke in, "Guess which one is Peter?"

"I'm afraid to!" Steven shot back.

"I'm Peter," the athletic-looking young man admitted. "And this is my wife, Nicole. I never tire of saying that!" he added as he kissed her lightly on the cheek.

The lithe, dark-skinned young woman, wearing a white turtleneck and black leotards, smiled and said hello in a silky soft voice.

"I haven't introduced myself," Steve said, slightly embarrassed.

"Wait, there are more: Karrie . . . Daniel . . . Emma. Come on in here. We have company!"

A young man, a woman, and a girl about Wellesley's age came from the doorway near the Christmas tree.

Julia completed her introduction. "This is my daughter Karrie, her husband Daniel, and their daughter—my *granddaughter*—Emma," she said proudly.

Steven finally got his chance. "I'm Steven Caufield, and this is my daughter, Wellesley," he said proudly, placing a hand on each of her shoulders.

"My, that is a very interesting name, Wellesley," Julia commented.

Wellesley was suddenly shy and didn't respond, so Steven stepped in. "It's from a book I read when I was a child," he began, but he was quickly interrupted.

"*Mars is Heaven*?" Daniel asked.

Steven was amazed. "Yes. I'm surprised you know it!"

The young man with the even younger beard smiled. "So, you're named after Wellesley!" he said, smiling at her.

"Who is Wellesley, dear?" Julia asked her son-in-law.

"Oh, it's not a person, it's a place. A *magical* place," he began. "It's a special, secret place you take someone who needs your help. You can grant them their fondest wish there."

"Kind of a fairy tale. My parents read it to me, and I read it to her," Steven said, still protectively holding her. "Mostly to help explain *why* we chose such a unique name."

"I'm sure she liked the name once she heard the story behind it," Daniel surmised.

"I think it's a cool name!" Emma spoke up.

Steven noticed a look of relief on Wellesley's face.

Julia held her hands to her mouth. "What am I doing? These people are still likely half frozen! There, go stand by the fire and warm yourself. And Emma and I have just the thing to *really* warm you up!"

Steven and Wellesley did as instructed, while Julia and Emma disappeared through the doorway. He quickly realized he didn't need to get too close to feel the wall of heat radiating back at him.

"We saw your lights coming down the laneway," Gene began. "We figured you'd be knocking at the door before long. Not a night out for man or beast!"

Steven agreed and relayed the story of their adventure: "The problem is, I'm stuck in a snowbank."

Julia and Emma emerged, presumably from the kitchen, carrying snowman-shaped mugs topped with whipped cream and chocolate sprinkles. Julia carefully passed them off to Wellesley and Steven.

"You're in luck! Get ready to have the best hot chocolate you've ever tasted!" Gene boasted.

Steven took a careful sip to test the temperature—it was perfect for drinking now. His eyes lit up when he realized he was savoring more than just the hot chocolate.

"What's in this?" he asked with a smile. "It's delicious!"

Julia smiled and whispered to him, "A little Verpooten—in yours, not Wellesley's." She smirked.

Steven was sure his expression showed he didn't know what she meant.

"It's German Advocaat. I'm glad you like it!"

"Goes *real* well with eggnog, too!" Gene added. "We'll have some of that later!"

Steven asked his daughter how she was enjoying hers. "It's excellent, Dad. Should we call Mom now and tell her what happened?"

Steven could almost hear his heart pause between beats. *Of course, they should call her.* He reached for his phone and was surprised to see no service. He looked around for Julia and saw her giving instructions to her daughter and son-in-law.

"May I use your phone?" he asked. "I need to call my wife and tell her what's happening."

Her face saddened as she bit her lip. "You can, but the lines must be down from the storm. We tried calling a while ago to see if church was canceled tonight. But we couldn't get through. You're welcome to try."

"I see. Do you have Wi-Fi?"

Julia nodded. "Uh huh, let me get Peter. He knows all about the electronic stuff. . . . Peter?"

The newlywed husband was chatting with his wife and Rob when he excused himself and came over.

"Peter, dear, can you show Steven here the Hi-Fi? We really should have music playing on Christmas Eve!"

"Sure thing!" he said, eagerly leading Steven to a large wooden cabinet. He opened the lid, and inside was a record player. Peter knelt and opened a door on the cabinet, revealing vinyl LP records leaning inside. He reached in and retrieved several.

"What would you like to hear? We have . . . *The Magic of Christmas: Nat King Cole, Christmas with Perry Como* . . . Johnny Cash: *The Classic Christmas Album.*"

Steven reached for the albums and examined their covers—they appeared to be in mint condition.

"You have that one at home!" Wellesley said, pointing to *The Magic of Christmas.*

"I do," Steven confirmed.

Wellesley had his attention. "Is it okay if Emma shows me around the Inn?"

"Sure," Steven replied. "Don't get lost."

He returned to reviewing the albums. "Impressive collection. They look almost new."

"Yeah, they are," Peter said. "So, which is it—Nat King Cole?"

"Sure," Steven agreed. He was still feeling the glow from the special ingredient in his hot chocolate.

"C'mon, Steve, have a seat over here with us. Take a load off!" Gene beckoned him. He did, finally feeling comfortable in the situation.

Steven nodded. "We shouldn't be imposing on your family's Christmas."

Gene laughed. "Our family Christmas? No, no. Our kids live halfway around the world. Australia. We wished them a Merry Christmas before the phone went down. No, we're guests here at the Inn."

Steven looked around the room, viewing it differently from when they had arrived.

"The Inn?"

"Sure. Since her husband passed away a few years ago, Julia runs the place now. We're guests here, like those newlywed kids and you and your daughter."

Chapter Four

Steven glanced at his watch: 6:31.

That can't be the correct time, he thought, but he noticed a grandfather clock to the left of the fireplace—it read the same time.

He finished his hot chocolate, put down the mug, and took in his surroundings for the first time. The furniture (wooden chairs and tables) was primarily colonial. The couch, loveseat, and lamps were more modern but still of an older, almost seventies style. Steven listened to Nat King Cole sing, "Here We Come a Caroling," concluding that the "Hi-Fi," as Julia had referred to it, must be from the sixties—though it looked new.

He then remembered his phone. Still no service. If the lines were repaired, he should be able to place a call. He searched the room for a phone—a rotary phone on a small table next to a floor lamp surprised him. He picked up the receiver, but there was no dial tone.

Julia suddenly appeared beside him. "As luck would have it, we have an empty room upstairs. We have a comfortable place for you to stay."

"Julia, it's wonderful for you to take us in like this. As you can appreciate, we didn't have a choice. We're very lucky . . ."

She smiled and stopped him midsentence. "*We* are lucky that we now have someone to fill an empty room. Dinner will be ready soon, and we have plenty, so please join us!"

Steven hadn't thought about dinner. It had been several hours since they'd had a snack at the highway rest stop.

Steven thanked her. "Okay then. Please add it to our bill."

"Oh, it's included in the twenty-five dollars!" she replied.

He blinked, astonished.

"*Twenty-five dollars?*" he said—a bit too loud but fortunately only heard by Julia.

She put her hand on his arm. "Is that too dear for a room?"

Steven shook his head. "No . . . no, it's just . . . how can you make any money charging only twenty-five for a room?"

She smiled and assured him, "We do fine, thank you." Julia repeated her news about dinner and disappeared into the dining room.

He was now officially curious about this place and how it worked, so he followed Julia to the entrance of a traditionally sized dining room. A long, wooden table with ten chairs filled most of the hardwood-floored room. At one end stood two tall glass-door cabinets, with a sideboard sandwiched between them. Pine garland laced with holly berries hung above the cabinet tops, held in place by white pillar candles. A white tablecloth runner stretched along the center of the table, showing off a modest centerpiece composed of pinecones and poinsettia flowers. Each place setting of silverware flanked a bone china plate. Opposite the silverware was a colored Christmas cracker. The quaint European tradition amused Steven.

He heard voices coming from the adjoining kitchen and enjoyed the delightful aroma of roast turkey and sage dressing. As his senses became overloaded with the spectacle, he felt a hand at his side.

He looked down to see Wellesley looking up at him. "We're staying here tonight, aren't we?" she said, more than asked, as if she were informing her father of the plan.

Steven wanted confirmation that Wellesley was accepting of their predicament. "Are you okay with it? I don't think we have a choice. No one would want to get our car out in this weather," he assured her.

"That's okay," she said.

"What have you been doing since we got here? I guess I lost track of you."

"No worries. Emma showed me around. Her room is on this floor. Our room is upstairs."

He was amazed, but not surprised, at how easily and quickly his daughter could adapt to new situations.

"I wish we could have gotten a message to your mom, though."

Wellesley agreed. "I know. They don't even have internet here."

That news didn't surprise Steven, given the place's throwback theme.

Julia stuck her head into the parlor and announced then: "Dinner, everyone!"

Peter and his wife let Gene and Bob pass, allowing the older couple to be seated first. Steven waited for the newlyweds to choose seats and stood until Daniel came in from the kitchen holding a large platter of carved meat.

"You folks can sit anywhere you like!" Daniel directed as he carefully placed the dish beside the centerpiece.

Julia, Karrie, and Emma followed behind like a parade of waitstaff, bringing bowls of dressing, vegetables, and potatoes and placing them around the table.

Gene surveyed the spread while taking inventory. "What? No gravy?" he asked.

Roberta slapped him on the arm and disapprovingly uttered, "GENE!"

"We didn't forget the gravy, Gene!" Daniel shot back as he placed a bowl of cranberry sauce beside Gene. "I knew you'd be the first to go for this!"

Gene smiled broadly and replied, "You know me too well!"

Julia appeared with the missing gravy, held up the bowl while glancing at Gene, then placed it at the end of the table furthest away from him.

"Serves you right, smarty!" Roberta scolded her husband.

Julia gathered everyone's attention. "Daniel will take your beverage orders. We have wine, and juice, and whatever else you fancy."

She noticed that Steven and Wellesley were still standing. "Have a seat, you two. Steven, you will sit at the end and Wellesley beside you."

They did as directed, and Emma came in, having done her serving chores, and sat beside Wellesley. They began chatting as if they were old friends.

Daniel was making the rounds, taking drink orders. His wife added the last dinner menu item to the table—a platter of freshly baked rolls wrapped in a white napkin.

Julia appeared at the head of the table, surveying it to ensure nothing was missing.

Once her son-in-law had served everyone, she said, "Thank you all for coming. We are so grateful to have you here with us on this *very* special night. It's wonderful to have a full house. And to Steven and Wellesley, we're so glad you are here, so we have no empty seats. It is an ancient tradition to have *one* seat empty at the table in case any lost soul needs a meal, and tonight we need not worry about that."

Steven smiled and said, "Thank you." Out of the corner of his eye, he noticed an empty chair in the corner he'd not seen before.

She continued. "We'll now say grace." She looked at Daniel on her left, and he began.

"Lord, thank you for the plentiful bounty you have provided, and the good health to enjoy it. We are grateful for one more time to celebrate with family . . . and friends . . . on this, the most special of nights, the birth of our savior and his love for us. With joy we say, Amen!"

The group repeated "Amen!" Steven couldn't remember the last time he had said *that*.

The serving dishes circulated the table, and the empty plates soon became crowded. Julia had prepared a honey-glazed ham and a roasted turkey. Mashed potatoes, butternut squash, bacon-coated Brussels sprouts, corn, and broccoli with cheese sauce gave their meal a kaleidoscope of flavors.

Gene was the first to raise his glass. "A toast, to our host," he declared as he stood up to clink his glass with all those within reach.

"Merry Christmas!" Roberta said, joining in.

"Everyone can open their crackers now!" Julia announced.

The dinner guests turned to the person on their right, as each held an end of the cracker, and counted, "One, two, three, PULL!"

Wellesley was disappointed that her cracker didn't pop, so Steven exchanged crackers with her. She then helped him pull his. He removed the gold foil from the cardboard tube, revealing a purple paper crown hat. He looked around the table, noticing most guests were already sporting their colorful party hats.

His search also revealed a plastic engagement ring with a marquee-cut "diamond" and a rolled-up message. The ring looked like a replica of the one he'd given April when he asked her to marry him. He was just about to read the message when his daughter noticed the ring.

"It looks like Mom's," she commented.

"It does, doesn't it," he agreed.

"You should give it to mom . . . for Christmas. You know, to remind her how much you love her."

Steven couldn't believe he was getting inadvertent marriage advice from his pre-teen daughter. He was about to ask her how she had come up with that when she asked him a question instead.

"Hey, Dad? What happened to the man who stole an Advent calendar?"

Steven shrugged his shoulders. She laughed and answered, "He got twenty-five days!"

He hugged Wellesley and unraveled his message, hoping it was as funny. It read, *Joy is what happens to us when we allow ourselves to recognize how good things really are. —Marianne Williamson*

Steven enjoyed the meal as if it were his last. Everything, from the savory meat to the warm and tender rolls, had an outpouring of flavor that raised his sense of taste to a higher level.

"This is wonderful!" he remarked, looking at Julia to commend her.

"Oh, go on, it's just a simple country dinner. I can't imagine what kind of fancy food you're used to in the city!"

Steven didn't recall having had a meal *this* good at any restaurant in Toronto. As he sipped his glass of perfectly dry and crisp white wine, it occurred to him he hadn't mentioned *where* he and Wellesley were from.

"So, where're you from, Steve?" Gene asked as the conversation picked up now that everyone was making progress on their meal.

"We live in Toronto, but we have a cottage on Clear Lake. That's where we were headed tonight."

"Well, you're not too far away. Shouldn't take you too long to get there in the morning if we can dig your car out." Gene chuckled.

Steven remembered their suitcases were still in the vehicle, but Daniel reassured him. "We'll deal with that after dinner."

Steven hadn't realized he'd spoken the concern aloud.

Julia looked around the table, making sure her guests were satisfied. "Don't be shy if you want seconds!" she said. Everyone appeared to be full, so she continued. "We will have a break and relax in the parlor. We'll have our dessert and coffee in there later."

When Julia stood up, Gene, Peter, and Daniel did so almost automatically—before Steven could even back up his chair to join them.

"Can I help tidy up in the kitchen?" Steven asked as the men left the room.

"Mercy sakes, no!" Julia fired back. "You are our guest. Relax!"

He nodded and reluctantly accompanied the others to the parlor. As the newlyweds approached him, he resumed his former place in front of the fire.

"We'd like to help you retrieve your things from your car," they offered.

"That's kind of you, but I will manage."

Nicole spoke first. "I've been looking outside. It's not snowing as much as before, but the wind has picked up. You can hear it if you stand near the front door. You may have to dig out around the car before you can get in."

Steven admitted he had not considered that part.

Peter reaffirmed his offer. "If we go out now, your things will warm before bedtime."

Steven knew Peter was right. He looked at his watch—7:25—and then immediately looked toward the grandfather clock. Grandpa agreed with the watch.

"How is this possible?" he asked himself.

"How is what possible?" Nicole asked him.

"It's not even seven thirty? It must've been at least seven when we sat for dinner?" Steven surmised.

"I don't know. . . . Was it?" Peter asked.

Steven forced himself to temporarily forget about this anomaly and decided to focus on the task at hand—going out in the storm.

"Okay. We'll go out. Let me talk to my daughter first." He went looking for Wellesley, but as soon as he turned, there she was, hurrying toward him with Emma.

"Is it okay if I make cookies with Emma?"

He nodded. "If it's okay with her mother. What kind of cookies?"

Emma answered, "Pepper-sneeze!"

"Pepper sneeze?" Steven repeated.

Karrie appeared with a dishtowel over her shoulder. "Emma? Are we baking cookies?"

"He said it's okay!" she answered.

"You're baking *pepper sneeze*?" Steven asked.

Karrie burst out laughing. "Not exactly. It's what Emma calls Pfeffernusse. They are a German spice cookie. Like gingerbread, but nicer."

"Ah. Go for it. As long as I get to taste them!" Steven agreed.

The kids were about to run to the kitchen when Steven asked Wellesley, "I'm going to the car. What do you need?"

"My backpack!" she called while running. "And suitcase!"

At the front door, Steven, Nicole, and Peter layered up as if they were preparing to trek to the North Pole.

"There's a shovel outside the door, and a broom," Peter said. "I can dig out while Nicole brushes the snow off, if it's possible in that wind."

"I guess we'll find out fast," Steven said.

Chapter Five

The wind hadn't died down, making it difficult to tell how much snow was still falling—most of it flying in the air was likely residual from the drifts. Steven borrowed a flashlight since his stranded vehicle was too far from the Inn's dim lights to receive much illumination.

The trio had to hop-skip through the deep snow to avoid being trapped. Only the driver's side windows weren't snow-covered when they reached the SUV. A white toque-shaped drift adorned the vehicle's roof, and the fenders seemed to sport wind-tunnel-tested white skirts.

Steven reached for his key fob and opened the doors. The lights blinked briefly, and the horn emitted a two-note chirp.

"What was that?" Peter asked, slightly alarmed by the noise.

"The security system," Steven said.

Nicole began brushing snow from the roof and doors but had to stop periodically and turn her head away from the wind to keep the snow from attacking her face. Her husband began digging, clearing behind the rear wheels. Steven cleared the hatch door and pulled on the handle. Once inside, he quickly fetched the luggage and slung Wellesley's backpack over one shoulder.

Peter remarked on the vehicle's shape, visible only whenever the flashlight revealed it.

"What kind of van *is* this?" he asked. He took the broom from Nicole, who'd offered to take the backpack from Steven.

Steven quickly closed the door and hit the remote to lock it, even though no one would likely venture out on this night to steal it.

"It's a Cadillac, XT-6," he answered as the three turned toward the house, thankful the wind was mostly behind them now.

"I've never heard of that," Peter replied.

When the rescuers returned to the Inn, they began shaking and stomping the residual snow onto the outdoor mat. Once inside, they wasted no time taking up positions in front of the fire.

"I appreciate your help," Steven told them as he began thawing his hands while rubbing them.

"We wouldn't feel right letting you go alone," Peter stated.

Steven remembered what he'd been told about their situation—newlyweds.

"So, congratulations are in order. I understand you are newly married."

Nicole smiled at her husband and gave him a warming peck on the cheek as she wrapped her hands around his upper arm and drew him closer to her.

"We were married yesterday." Peter smiled as Nicole put her head on his shoulder.

"Really? The twenty-third? That's our anniversary too."

"No kidding?' Nicole asked.

Steven had to qualify his statement. "I'd better explain. December twenty-third is the anniversary of when we were *engaged*. But we celebrate it like our actual wedding anniversary in October."

"That's sweet!" Nicole said.

Steven now recalled this year's anniversary—the one that wasn't. Every year since they were engaged, he and April returned to the same restaurant in Markham, where they'd had dinner the evening he proposed to April.

Peter asked, "How long have you been married?"

"Thirteen years." He answered automatically. It made him wonder for the first time if there would be a fourteenth. His thoughts focused on April. He knew she would be concerned about Wellesley's absence—he wasn't sure how she felt about *his*.

Steven remembered how much he loved holding April, feeling her warmth and the fragrance of her hair. He missed her and wanted to be with her now. It wouldn't happen tonight, but he'd talk with her tomorrow. He had to know what she was thinking.

"Anybody ready for dessert?" Gene shouted out.

He entered from the dining room, holding a plate in one hand and a cup of coffee in the other.

Julia appeared after him, wiping her hands on her apron and scolding Gene. "Now I told you to *wait* for the others!"

Gene acted like a kid who had swiped some candy from the store. He scooted across the large room and plopped himself onto the loveseat. "Every man for himself!" he declared.

Julia sighed. "Come in the dining room, everyone. We have coffee and tea ready."

Steven followed the newlyweds in and noticed Roberta helping the girls put their freshly baked cookies on a platter.

Julia drew everyone's attention to the dining room table, which was buffet-style for dessert. "We have apple pie, vanilla ice cream if you so choose, christstollen, apple strudel. And the girls have made their pfeffernusse cookies. On the sideboard, we have coffee and tea or hot chocolate. Everyone—help yourselves!"

A piece of the deep-dish apple pie, courtesy of Gene, was missing. While Steven debated his choices, Wellesley and Emma ran up to him.

"Try our cookies, Dad!" Wellesley demanded as she hugged her father around the waist.

"You made these?" Steven teased.

"She's great in the kitchen!" Emma praised her.

"I'm not surprised," Steven said. "She makes cookies with her mom . . . all the time."

Wellesley smiled in agreement. But it was easy to tell she missed her mother as much as Steven did. The girls sampled their masterpiece, making room for ice cream and hot chocolate. Steven was surprised at how good the cookies were.

"You've never had them before?" Emma asked him as if he were a cookie pilgrim.

"I have not," he admitted.

Julia overheard the conversation. "Have you had christstollen?"

He shook his head shamefully.

"Well, you *must*! It isn't Christmas without it!" she said, slicing a large piece from the loaf and placing it on the plate she handed him. "It goes very well with coffee."

Julia had understated her suggestion—it went very well *without* coffee, too, as he found out when he returned for seconds. The flaky, icing sugar–dusted pastry held the moist flavor of spices, rum, raisins, and candied fruit.

When everyone was kicking back, enjoying the warmth of the fire and the friendly conversation, Julia delivered some news. "After a big meal and dessert, we usually go for a long walk in the snow. Well, looking outside, that's not the best plan for tonight. So, I suggest we sing instead of working off our meal."

Gene and Roberta were up in a jiffy as if sprung. "Ready to go!" they said in unison.

Julia passed some well-worn lyric sheets and said, "And I think we have a piano player in our group," looking in Nicole's direction.

Nicole tugged at her white turtleneck as if embarrassed. "Up you go, my dear!" her husband encouraged as he lifted his wife like a groom ready to cross a threshold.

"Ahhh, put me down!" she protested, and he granted her wish. She strolled up to the piano, sat on the bench, and tested it for a tune. Nicole glanced through the songbook and asked, "What shall we sing?"

"Hark the Herald!" Emma yelled out.

Nicole scanned the pages until she found it. Peter was now by her side, proudly admiring his bride.

Julia called for her daughter and son-in-law to come in from the kitchen, and Karrie and Daniel joined the circle with their daughter in front of them.

Wellesley was reluctant to join in, so Steven took her by the hand, but she preferred to take a space beside Emma.

Gene was ready to lead the chorus. "And a one, and a two, and a THREE!"

The group burst into song, and the nine voices sounded like a choir—perhaps not a *well-practiced* choir, but a choir. Nicole was concentrating on her playing and didn't sing along. After the first of many songs, Peter had to correct that.

"Honey, you have such a wonderful voice, you *have* to sing!"

She muttered something to him, but he wouldn't stop.

"Here, let me," he said, offering to take her place. "I only know how to play one song: 'Silent Night.'" He exchanged places with Nicole, and she took a deep breath as he began playing.

When she sang the first "Silent Night," it was as if an angel had entered the room. Everyone who joined in at the beginning paused, one by one, to hear her sing solo. Nicole raised her hands, beckoning everyone to join in the second verse, and some did. In contrast, others silently admired the beautiful sound of her voice.

Nicole finished to a round of applause. Peter gave her a congratulatory hug, and she took up her place on the piano bench. "So, what's next?" she asked.

"Joy to the World!" Roberta shouted.

The group searched for the song on their pages while Nicole found the sheet music. Steven noticed the large crèche taking up a pine shelf above the piano as she played the chords for the first chorus. Colorful figurines of Mary and Joseph surrounded the baby Jesus, while the three kings stood by in admiration. It reminded him of a smaller nativity scene in his childhood home. He glanced at his watch: 8:10. Once again, he looked to grandfather for confirmation, and the clock face confirmed it. Steven couldn't understand that.

"I thought time is supposed to *fly* when you're having fun," he mumbled to himself.

He hadn't realized he'd spoken loudly enough to be heard, but then Julia asked, "Did I hear you say you're having fun?"

Steven was surprised—he also hadn't realized she was within earshot.

"We are. It's just, well, it seems time passes very *slowly* here. I know it's a ridiculous thing to say, but . . ."

Julia smiled. "Not at all. We are so glad to have you, and we want it to last as long as possible!"

Steven wondered what she meant by that.

Daniel appeared carrying a large leather firewood tote and began stacking the firewood in the log box. Karrie followed behind him, carrying an armload of gifts wrapped in shiny paper, tied with colored ribbon, and topped with contrasting-colored bows. She carefully arranged them below the large Christmas tree.

"We'll be opening gifts soon," Julia announced.

Steven remembered he had a gift for Wellesley in his suitcase and approached Julia then. "Can you direct me to our room? I need to get Wellesley's gift from my suitcase."

Julia grinned, almost laughing. "I can. It's the second door on your right, at the top of the stairs. But you don't need to give it to her now. There is a gift under the tree for her—and you."

He looked at her in amazement. "How did you . . .?" He couldn't find words to finish the sentence.

Julia's gray-blue eyes sparkled as she said, "We can't think of everything, but we try!"

Chapter Six

"We do things differently here—in the old German style. We open our gifts on Christmas Eve, the same night the three kings gave their gifts to the baby Jesus. Gather 'round, everyone. Everyone takes a seat. Daniel will play Santa Claus," she said. Her son-in-law now sported a Santa cap.

Wellesley suddenly seemed shy about the proceedings. She approached Steven and said, "We don't have any gifts for anyone."

Steven put his hands on her shoulders and looked her in the eye. "Sweetheart, no one is expecting us to. No one expected us *to be here* tonight. It'll be okay, you'll see."

She seemed to accept Steven's outlook for now and tucked her long hair behind one ear as she sat on the large rug in front of him. Daniel continued retrieving gifts from under the tree and distributing them to their recipients.

"Go ahead, Roberta, you begin!" Julia instructed.

Roberta put on her glasses and let them rest on the bridge of her nose while she carefully separated the paper where the tape joined the seams as if she were going to save it.

"For corn sakes, woman, just rip it open!" Gene barked.

Roberta, clearly used to paying no attention to his outbursts, continued to carefully reveal the package's contents—a wool-knitted sweater with a montage of red reindeer and white snowflakes. "It's gorgeous!" she exclaimed as she thanked everyone.

Gene went next and wasted no time, tearing into his package as if to show how it should be done. "Well, lookee here . . . cigars. From Cuba, no less. How did you know?" he asked, passing one under his nose to verify its quality.

Julia held her hands in her lap and smiled. "Santa knows. It must have been on your list!"

Nicole went next, and her package was small—not much bigger than a juice box. She unwrapped it cautiously and looked at Peter, who didn't know what was inside. Under the holiday-themed wrapping paper was a Robin's egg blue box, tied with a ribbon with the initials HB on the lid. She carefully removed the lid. Inside, resting on a snow-colored bed of cotton, was a silver chain with a heart-shaped pendant attached.

"It's lovely!" she declared and moved to give Peter a hug and kiss.

He accepted the praise, but quickly added, "I'll take that. But I'm not the one responsible." Nicole noticed the tag on the wrapping, which read, *To: Nicole From: Santa Claus.*

"Thank you, Santa," she giggled, and Peter helped her place it around her neck.

Her husband was next, and the package with a PETER nametag surprised him. Unraveling soon revealed a box emblazoned with a large Canadian Tire logo. He broke open the lid and discovered it contained a two-person tent. His smile was unbreakable. "This is just the thing for our camping trips next summer," Peter exclaimed.

Santa Daniel continued his rounds, stopping with packages for Wellesley and Steven. Steven had to encourage his daughter to open the gift. Emma was nearby to help. Wellesley opened the package in seconds but wasn't sure what to make of it.

"It's UNO, a card game. You can play it with three people," Emma explained.

Julia stood beside her granddaughter and said, "This is something you and your parents can play together."

"It's perfect!" Wellesley proclaimed, looking at her father for his reaction, but Steven was not as optimistic—he couldn't picture them playing as a family in their present situation.

The girls quickly retreated to the large rug before the fire as Emma reviewed the game's rules.

"You're next," Daniel said, handing Steven a large, thin parcel. Steven carefully separated the paper as if he would damage whatever was inside. He held a watercolor painting of the Inn—a view of the exterior, from the viewpoint of the road. It was how the Inn *would* have looked had it been daylight and without the snowstorm. A red horse-drawn sleigh stood where his car would have been. Inside it were two figures, looking surprisingly like Steven and Wellesley, bundled up with a large blanket over them. They appeared to be waving in the artist's direction. Brightly colored wreaths and garlands decorated the Inn, and icicles hung from the eaves.

"I don't know what to say!" Steven began. "We don't have gifts for you."

Julia stood as she explained. "It is a little tradition we do here at the Inn."

Steven was bewildered. "What about you and your family? Don't you exchange gifts?"

"We do," she smiled. "But not tonight. We'll come home and open ours tomorrow morning after breakfast and church. Christmas Eve is for our guests."

Steven comprehended this, and he absentmindedly glanced at his watch: 9:30. He couldn't understand the time lapse. He felt like they'd been there all day—in reality, it had only been about three hours, according to his watch and grandfather in the corner.

Julia must've noticed his attention to time. "We normally get to bed a bit early on Christmas Eve. It is bedtime for Emma."

Steven looked over at the girls, and it was clear that Emma had heard her grandmother's remark. To Emma's credit, there was no pushback or whining about the curfew. Steven realized it was also good for Wellesley to call it a night.

"C'mon, kid!" he directed. Despite her protests, he knew Wellesley was tired from her long day.

Steven accompanied his daughter to their room on the second floor. He recalled when he used to carry her piggyback up the stairs, even taking two at a time when she was *very* young, to hear her shriek joyfully. He stopped in the doorway to flick on the light switch. They said, "Wow!" in unison at the pale mint-green, tastefully decorated room with silver and black accents. Someone had brought up their luggage and turned down the two double beds. A red and green–wrapped chocolate truffle sat on the trimmed pillow of each.

"Can I have mine now?" she asked.

"Sure, but brush your teeth after," he instructed. Wellesley headed down the hall to the washroom. At the same time, Steven unpacked a few things, leaving the gift he'd brought for Wellesley in the suitcase. *At least now I have something to give her in the morning*, he thought.

Wellesley returned from the washroom, now wearing her pajamas and carrying her clothes. Steven tucked her in and kissed her, saying, "Good night, kid. Sweet dreams." Wellesley smiled broadly, looking happier than he'd seen her in a long time.

"This is a *very* cool place, isn't it, Dad? Maybe we can come back here sometime with Mom?"

"That would be great!" he agreed, wondering if it could ever happen. He reached the doorway and heard laughter from downstairs, so he closed the bedroom door.

When Steven entered the parlor, he realized he'd heard the punchline to a joke Gene had been telling and knew from the groans that it was bad. Peter sat on the loveseat, with Nicole curled up close beside him. Roberta sat beside her husband on the couch. Steven pulled up a single chair to complete the company.

The conversation was varied. Gene told stories—mostly about his days owning a business that manufactured and installed windows. Roberta regularly stopped him, urging him to let someone *else* talk. He took the hint, asking Peter, "What do you do, son?"

Peter proudly said, "I'm a teacher. Elementary school, science and phys ed."

Gene nodded in approval while Peter continued. "Nicole teaches music at a private school."

Julia appeared in the doorway just as Gene was about to ask Steven what he did for a living.

"Would anyone care for a nightcap? Eggnog . . . Tom and Jerry . . . hot buttered rum. We have herbal tea—just the thing to help you sleep!"

"I don't think I'll need help," Steven admitted.

"You have to try the eggnog—they make it here!" Gene advised him.

Steven had only *heard* about the Tom and Jerry mix—he'd never tried it. He struggled to remember what movie he'd seen it in—*The Apartment*, perhaps?

"Give him eggnog," Gene said, placing Steven's order. "You won't regret it!"

Julia disappeared into the kitchen, and the conversation resumed as they finally grilled Steven about his vocation.

"Advertising," he announced.

"So, you are the one responsible for the annoying commercials that interrupt my shows?" Roberta chuckled.

Steven grinned slyly. "Not me personally. We only produce the ones that *aren't* annoying. Without them, television wouldn't be free. I used to be the guy who thought up ways to help you sell your windows, or to get people to send their kids to Nicole's school. I spend most of my time now entertaining clients, swaying them to spend their money with us."

"Sounds like a salesman to me," Gene concluded. "You like that, do you?"

"I used to love it." Steven admitted, "But lately . . ."

He didn't finish the thought as Julia appeared with the drinks, and after a brief toast, Steven got to try the eggnog.

"You've been building this up pretty well, Gene. It's obvious you were a superb salesman," Steven said, sipping the cinnamon, nutmeg, cream, and egg mixture—they came together in a symphony of flavors.

"I *still* am a good salesman!" Gene bragged.

"That may be, but this stuff sells itself. Best eggnog I've ever had!" Steven admitted.

Gene chuckled. "First, it's homemade, but it's the eighteen-year-old Jamaican rum that makes it. It's subtle at first—then after a while, it comes out of hiding to say, Merry Christmas!"

Steven nodded and looked over at the fire, which was larger and warmer than at any time that evening. He felt sleepy for the first time. It wasn't like him to tire out so early.

Julia, her daughter, and son-in-law entered the room together and sat near the fire. "Time to relax?" Steven asked, observing how hard the seemingly tireless grandmother had been working to entertain this group.

Steven suppressed an enormous yawn but wasn't successful. "My apologies," he said, covering his mouth. "It must be time for me to turn in."

"The rum got ya, did it?" Gene cackled.

"I guess." Steven agreed. "It's been a long day for us. I think I'll say goodnight, everyone," he said, and he struggled to get to his feet.

Julia stood up beside him and wished him sweet dreams. "Breakfast starts at eight, but if you like to sleep in a bit, we will save some for you."

Steven remembered his mission—to deliver Wellesley to her mother. "I don't want to be ungrateful, but we must leave in the morning. My wife . . ."

Julia clapped her hands together. "Of course, what am I thinking? But can your car go, or is it still stuck in the snow?"

Steven admitted he didn't know—the rescue team had been primarily interested in retrieving the bags and didn't spend as much time clearing a path.

"We'll get you out in the morning, don't you worry," Daniel said.

Julia nodded. Everyone was in on the plan except Steven, it seemed.

Chapter Seven

Steven rolled over onto his back. Bright sunlight was forcing its way between the wooden blinds. He could detect enough of the world outside to see part of a vivid blue sky. The thought of getting up now wasn't a pleasant one. The mattress was a perfect marriage between supple and firm, and the down-filled pillow was so comfortably cool that he didn't want to move his head. He leaned on one elbow as he put the previous day's events together. *The snowstorm*, he thought, explaining how he came to be where he was. He looked at the double bed beside him, which was empty. It was made, and Wellesley's backpack sat there upright.

His watch read 8:30, and again, he suspected its accuracy—it meant he'd slept for about ten hours, something he had not done since he was a teenager.

The bedroom door was closed, so he quickly dressed and went downstairs with their luggage to discover what was happening. He hadn't reached the bottom of the stairs before the aroma of bacon overcame him. He heard it sizzle. Daylight washed through the white-paneled parlor, which was vacant. He heard voices from the dining room and discovered it was full of guests.

"Merry Christmas, sleepy head!" Gene grinned, holding up a glass of orange juice as if he were toasting.

"Merry Christmas, everyone," Steven replied. The guests returned his wishes in unison. Wellesley sat beside Emma, and the two girls were comparing notes, likely on something parents weren't supposed to be privy to.

Julia entered the dining room carrying a basket of freshly baked pastries. She noticed Steven and directed him to a seat.

Steven nodded, approached her, and said, "Thank you for everything, Julia, but we should be on our way. Wellesley's mother will be worried. She hasn't heard from us since just before we arrived here."

She wiped her hands on the apron and said, "We understand. Wellesley was up early with Emma, so she had breakfast. "

"Thank you." He smiled.

Julia continued to be an uncommon host. "Daniel has a plan to get you going. Why don't you go to the barn and see what he's doing? You'll have time for some eggs, bacon, and a cup of coffee."

Steven had forgotten the condition of his SUV. When they retrieved the luggage the night before, snow was still falling, so he didn't know what condition it was in now.

Julia gave him directions. "Go down the hall and turn right. The door at the end leads to the garage. Go through the garage, and you'll see the barn."

He put on his coat and boots and followed her instructions. The enormous garage held a pickup truck and a van. As he passed, their pristine condition amazed him, considering their age. He was no expert on vintage trucks, but he estimated they were valuable. As he closed the garage door behind him, he noticed a large John Deere tractor with a snowplow fixed to its front. Steven thought the Inn appeared equipped to manage anything. Someone had plowed the area around the tractor since the storm.

Steven opened the door to the barn, greeted by the pungent smell of horse manure. He saw a man dressed in coveralls stuffed into black rubber boots. He wore a black and red plaid hunting cap, its ear flaps pulled down the side, and appeared to be opening the stall to let out a horse.

"Daniel?" Steven called out, and the man turned around.

"Good morning," Daniel called back. "You're just in time to help."

Steven rushed over and asked, "What do you need?"

Before Daniel continued, he felt introductions were in order. "This here is Thelma. She's one of our two Percherons. The one over there is Louise."

Daniel instructed Steven to hold up one end of the harness while he attached the other to their collars.

Steven shook his head. "I assume you named them after the movie!"

Daniel's face went blank. "The movie? They made a movie about Percherons?"

Steven was now confused. "No. I thought—no . . . It's not important." He let the comment pass; it was possible country folk weren't up to date with iconic films.

Daniel led the pair out of the barn after instructing Steven to open the large doors. Outside the barn sat a large, red wooden sleigh with *Hollidays' Inn* painted in gold lettering on the side.

"Are you getting ready for a sleigh ride?" Steven asked.

"Later," Daniel answered. "First, we have to get your buggy out of that drift."

Daniel continued dressing the draft horses in their pulling gear, stood behind them, snapped the reins, and yelled, "Go, girls!"

The two giant animals started together as Daniel directed them down the plowed driveway and onto the road.

"Wouldn't the tractor be easier?" Steve asked, hurrying beside Daniel as the horses picked up their pace.

"Maybe!" Daniel answered. "But not safer, at least not for your vehicle. These girls are strong but also gentle. They know how much to pull—no matter what." Daniel drove the team parallel to the rear of the SUV and prepared to wind the heavy nylon rope around the axle.

"It's a front-wheel drive, so there is no rear axle. You'll have to attach it to the trailer hitch, and I'll have to start the engine and put it in reverse; otherwise, you'll damage the transmission," Steven advised.

"You don't say!" Daniel said, giving his head a scratch. He waited for Steven's signal and gave the reins a flick, yelling, "Pull!" The horses lowered their heads and drove forward together. They had taken only a few steps before the SUV was free of its tunnel of snow.

"How about that?" Daniel asked, clapping his hands in victory. "Those girls always come through. Why'd ya think they call it horsepower anyway?"

Steven didn't have to guess. He was grateful that the vehicle was ready to continue their journey. He hurried into the Inn as Daniel returned the girls to the barn. "We're good to go!" he proclaimed to Julia.

"Are you sure I can't persuade you to have breakfast before you go?" she asked, with a look of mild disappointment on her face.

"I promise we'll be back. Wellesley suggested her mother would love to stay here. I think it will be just the thing for a gift; perhaps for Valentine's Day."

Julia smiled. "We'll be here. I'll keep a room open for you."

Stephen reached into his wallet and produced a credit card. Julia suddenly looked worried. "Oh, my dear, I'm afraid we don't have a machine for those. The bank keeps telling me we should get one."

Steven felt embarrassed, but he was sure he had cash. "Here you go," he said, handing her a fifty-dollar bill.

"Oh, let me get your change."

Steven reached for her arm to prevent her from rushing away.

"That's not necessary. You took us in when we had nowhere to go. You fed us and gave us a Christmas we'll never forget. Daniel even pulled my vehicle out of the snow—that alone is worth it. I am thankful for everything!"

Julia stood there, seemingly at a loss for words. At first, Steven thought he saw a tear welling up, but she wiped her eyes to prevent it and said, "You made *our* Christmas incredibly special. We thank *you* for that."

Steve followed Julia into the parlor, where the guests assembled.

"Everyone, Steven and Wellesley have to be on their way. I'm sure you'll join me in wishing them a Merry Christmas!" One by one, the guests and Julia's family lined up and offered their best wishes, either with handshakes, hugs, or, in Gene's case, both.

"Drive careful, son—and stay outta those snow banks!" he advised.

Julia ensured they didn't forget their gifts and handed Steven a canvas sack. "I put a tin in there, too, with some cookies the girls made."

Steven took a deep breath and thanked her again. He and Wellesley said their goodbyes, and as they stood beside the SUV, placing their luggage inside it and preparing to drive away, they noticed the entire group assembled on the front porch waving farewell.

Steven grabbed his sunglasses as he pulled onto the road, the sunlight reflecting off the plowed surface causing him to lose his vision. "You should check and see if we have service. I should have thought of that before we left," he told Wellesley.

"We didn't . . . but we do now!" she informed him. "I'll text Mom."

Usually, he'd call himself, but Steven was sticking to the *new* communication plan, going through their daughter. Unsurprisingly, they saw no vehicles on the road this Christmas morning.

Chapter Eight

Steven's anxiety was rising as he turned off Highway 28 and headed east on Sandy Point Road when Wellesley asked him a question.

"Dad, is it true that if you make a wish and tell what you wished for . . . that it won't come true?"

The question caught him off guard, and he changed his focus to something more positive. "I don't know, sweetheart. That's just an old wives' tale. But, if you want to play it safe, keep it a secret, just in case."

Wellesley appreciated his advice. He added, "If it *comes* true, you will be okay to share it, but people may not believe you. That's a small price to pay for getting your wish." She nodded her head in agreement.

Steven approached the driveway to his in-laws' cottage and was surprised to see it plowed. His father-in-law was notorious for not doing that in a timely fashion. When he stopped the SUV, Wellesley sprang out of the vehicle like it was on fire, leaving Steven to collect their luggage. April was standing on the porch, not wearing a coat, with her arms folded to keep out the chill. She quickly spread her arms, hugging her daughter as they disappeared into the cottage. Steven had to pause and put down the bags before letting himself in.

Once inside, he dropped his burden and removed his coat. His in-laws were drawn like magnets to Wellesley, smothering their granddaughter with hugs and kisses.

"Merry Christmas, honey!" The grandparents took turns wishing her as they bombarded her with questions.

Steven appeared, unacknowledged, in the living room.

April turned her attention to him then. She casually walked over to him, and he imagined that she was unsure if he was the husband who would enjoy Christmas with them or the one who had abandoned it (and his family) only a few weeks ago.

"Are you okay?" she asked.

"I think so. Last night had me wondering if I was," he replied.

"I was relieved to get your text last night," she began, "considering we haven't spoken in about a week."

Steven apologized for his silence and then considered the first part of her comment. He didn't know what she meant and told her so. He described the previous night's events to her and explained how their service had been interrupted.

"You texted me last night," she said, producing her phone to show him the message: The roads are terrible, and the bridge is closed at South Beach. We're spending the night at an inn. See you in the morning. The sent time was 6:31.

Steven recalled looking at his watch around that time, but they were inside the Inn without service by then.

"I'll try and explain, but it won't be easy."

She came closer and put her arms around his shoulders. "I'm impressed that you remembered the roasting pan. I can't tell if it's the real Steven I have back today, but you're here, and that's what matters, as long as you don't disappear again."

"After last night, I'm not going anywhere without you."

She half smiled and took his hand. "We can talk about this later. C'mon, let's spend Christmas with our family."

Christmas celebrations continued for the next few hours, as it usually did at the cottage. They opened gifts, snacked on treats, and April's father poured wine like water. April and her mother continued preparing dinner while her father and Wellesley worked on a jigsaw puzzle he'd started.

"So, you stayed at the Holiday Inn last night," April's dad began the interrogation.

"We did," Steven admitted, taking a sip of the Scotch that his father-in-law raved about.

"Long way to go, to Peterborough, to find a hotel. Was the Bridge Inn booked up?"

Steven stared into the glowing bed of orange coals beneath the log holder. "We didn't have to go that far. We were lucky to find a place by accident—just off 20. My mistake—they call it Hollidays' Inn, so they don't get sued. It's more like a B&B."

His father-in-law suddenly turned toward Steven and asked, "Someone reopened that old mausoleum? The original burned down fifty years ago. The family that owned it and some guests died in the fire. It was on Christmas Eve. The place had this enormous fireplace, which they used to heat part of the Inn. The fire department said it got clogged or something. That was about the second Christmas we spent up here. What a tragedy."

His father-in-law continued, "Ellie knew some of them." He called his wife.

"Ellie . . . what was the name of that Holliday woman that used to own the Inn?"

She heard the question and thought about it for a second before answering. "Julia . . . we knew her as Julia Alt *before* she married John Holliday. Why are you asking about her?"

Her husband was about to answer when Steven stopped him. "No, let it go. Obviously, I'm mistaken."

Wellesley appeared from the kitchen, obviously having overheard their exchange. "Dad, did you bring in the bag from the car that had my game in it . . . and the cookies?"

Steven's eyes went wide. He'd forgotten about the canvas bag that held the gifts and the treats, but surely something in there would be evidence of where they'd spent the night. He didn't remember bringing it in from the SUV, so he quickly checked the car but returned to the cottage without the bag.

"I don't remember putting it in the car. I think I left the bag on the road." He wasn't speaking to anyone but himself, but April was within earshot, so she asked him to repeat it. She stopped him right there when he told her he was going for a drive to confirm his suspicion.

"You aren't going *anywhere* without me, mister—remember?" she said, putting on her coat and boots. "And give me the keys. I'll drive. You just finished a scotch."

"I didn't finish it, but I won't object."

April informed her parents they'd be back before dinner, and shortly after, they set off down the sunlit Route 20.

"You need to tell me where to turn," she said, slowing down and looking for a side road or driveway. The vehicle navigator was working now.

The SUV was practically crawling when he shouted, "Stop here, April!"

She parked the vehicle, and they both got out.

Steven didn't answer—instead, he looked off into the distance where, earlier that morning, a porch had stood on which eight people had waved them goodbye. There was nothing but snowdrifts where the Inn should be. He had been contemplating this when April appeared by his side.

"You stayed here last night? Where is the inn?"

Steven looked left and right, scanning the area as if a white clapboard building would spring up. It did not.

"I set the trip navigator when we left here . . . and this is exactly where we started from this morning. I don't get it."

April was amazed. "You don't get it? Is this some sort of joke between you and Wellesley?"

Steven shook his head. "That's for April Fools, not Christmas. I know there was an inn, right here, where we stayed last night. We had a wonderful time."

He looked around on the road for the canvas bag that held the gifts and cookies, hoping that would help corroborate his story—he found nothing.

"You clearly had a long night and are still out of it. Let's just go back. There's something else I need to ask you," she told him.

On the drive back to the cottage, they discussed his departure. "I was wrong to leave. And I was wrong to allow business to come between my family and me—especially at Christmas. That was something I was reminded of last night."

"How so?" April asked.

"Being with other families who were enjoying each other's company. It reminded me of how much I missed you."

Steven thought he saw a smile appear on April's face. He adjusted his seat belt for comfort and touched something in his pocket. He found a plastic ring and suddenly remembered where it came from—the Christmas cracker.

"Look at this!" he exclaimed.

She took her attention away from the road for a second and laughed. "It looks like a plastic copy of my ring. Where'd you get it?"

Steven told her about Christmas dinner the night before. He was still looking at her as they turned into the cottage driveway. When she stopped the vehicle, he presented her with the ring and quoted part of his wedding vows: "I give you this ring as a symbol of my love for you."

She accepted it, reached for his face with both hands, and gently kissed him. "Glad to have you back."

Once inside the cottage, they were removing their coats and boots when Wellesley appeared. "Look what I found online!" she said while handing an iPad to her dad.

Steven saw an image of the watercolor painting he was gifted on Christmas Eve, the same one that had been in the canvas bag he'd somehow lost.

"That's it!" Steven exclaimed.

His father-in-law confirmed it with a nod. "Yeah, that's what it used to look like."

"Did you find the bag?" Wellesley asked.

"It wasn't there, honey. I'm afraid no one will ever believe us about where we stayed last night," he said, tossing a look at his father-in-law, who waved him off.

Steven then observed Wellesley notice her mother's right hand, on which a plastic ring mirrored the one on her left hand.

"The ring!" Wellesley shouted. "You gave Mom the ring from the cracker. Doesn't that prove it?"

"Not much proof, but that *is* where it came from," he agreed.

Wellesley shook her head and said, "Maybe it doesn't prove that the Inn was real, but it does prove that wishes come true . . . especially at Christmas."

"That's right, honey," her mom told her. "You might have experienced your own Wellesley last night . . . just like in *Mars Is Heaven*."

Steven looked at April and added, "And you and I have our own little Wellesley, right here."

About the Author

Rick Ferguson lives in Uxbridge, Ontario, with his wife Terry and dog Ellie. Now retired from a forty-six-year career as a sheet metal worker and estimator, he spends his time with his true passion: writing fiction.

Rick self-published his first novel, *The Ghosts in Maple Leaf Gardens*, with iUniverse in 2013. The story is about Dale McCaine, a young player who was denied a chance to play for the Leafs, and the curse on the team that prevents them from winning the Stanley Cup. The ghosts of five former Leaf greats arrive to help end the curse for the team's long-suffering fans.

You can find Rick on Instagram:
@rickfergusonauthor

To learn more about Rick, visit his website at:
www.readingintuit.ca

The
Kindness
Challenge

The Kindness Challenge

Melissa Cate

The smells of the day before still lingered. Pumpkin, cinnamon, cranberry, turkey. They mingled in the air, and Leah drew a deep breath, savoring the comfort they brought. She sat alone at the breakfast nook, her fingers wrapped around a mug of coffee. Tears sprung to her eyes as she glimpsed the book lying open on the table.

In a few days, she would continue a tradition her children enjoyed every December. Twenty-five days of kindness. Sometimes random. Sometimes not so random. This year had to look different, even if her little loves didn't understand that. Even if she didn't know how yet. She drew the mug to her mouth, sipped at the energy-giving liquid and hoped it would give her brain a jolt. She blinked as an idea flashed in her mind's eye. She began making notes in her book, coffee forgotten as ideas began to take shape, ways for her to feel like her husband was home for the holidays.

December 1

Dear Lucy and Micah,
You've had a big change this year. Let's kick off 25 Days of Kindness by picking up some of your daddy's favorite donuts and taking them to his work to surprise his coworkers.
Love,
Mama

Leah smiled as her children walked into Ark8 Design, carrying boxes from the local bakery. She spied the receptionist, Brenda, finishing up a phone call before greeting them.

"Hi, Lucy! Hi, Micah! What brings y'all in today?" She walked around her desk. "I'm so glad to see you three," she whispered as she hugged Leah.

"We brought Daddy's favorite donuts to share with everyone." Despite her matter-of-fact response, Brenda noticed the tears in Lucy's eyes as she bit her lip.

"That was mighty nice of you, sweetheart. Would you like to take them to the offices, or would you like to put them in the breakroom?"

Nine-year-old Micah shrugged as he looked at his sister. Lucy's eyes widened as she glanced at Leah to answer.

"I think they'd like to visit a couple of offices, but leave the rest," answered Leah. Lucy nodded in agreement.

Brenda's gaze softened. "Certainly. You know where everyone is."

"Thank you." Leah started toward the back, turning when she noticed Micah hadn't followed.

Micah tilted his head toward Brenda. Leah grinned. "Would you like an apple fritter, Brenda?"

"I'd love one, thank you." She helped Micah with the box and set a fritter on her desk. She knelt down to his level. "This was very sweet of you, Micah."

Micah blushed and hurried off with his mom.

December 2

Dear Lucy and Micah,

I'm so proud of you. You did a great job handing out apple fritters yesterday. Your daddy was a great artist. Today, I would like for you to each make at least two pictures for us to take to some of the seniors in our neighborhood. We'll deliver them later this week.

Love,
Mama

Lucy's tongue stuck out of the side of her mouth as she concentrated on her second drawing. Micah had finished and was eating some goldfish. He bent over Lucy to look at her picture.

"Micah! You got crumbs on my picture!" The tween burst into tears as she yelled for her mom.

"I'm sorry! I just wanted to see it!" Micah erupted in tears.

Leah walked in and hugged the youngsters. They collapsed into a heap on the floor, hugging and crying together.

"I miss our drawing contests," wailed Lucy, tears streaming down her face.

"I know, sweetheart," whispered Leah, rubbing Lucy's back.

"I miss Daddy," cried Micah.

Leah pulled her son close. "Me too, bubba, me too."

In that moment, she recognized having something every day might be too much this year and made a mental note to change their kindness challenges for a few days.

December 5

Dear Lucy and Micah,

You have done wonderfully the past few days, delivering candy canes to people who helped you at stores and giving stickers to your friends at school. Today, let's make some of Daddy's favorite cookies to deliver with the pictures you made.

Love,
Mama

"Remember how daddy tries—tried—to eat all the frosting before we could put them on the cookies?" Lucy giggled.

"And Mommy always told him no cookie dough." Micah laughed as he remembered. "That's why he'd eat the frosting."

"That, and it's *yummy*!" Lucy leaned into Leah. "So. Yummy."

Leah grinned as she wiped the flour from her daughter's nose and swiped it across Micah's cheek. "You have a little something on your cheek, bubs."

Micah stuck his finger in the bowl beside him and rubbed it against Leah's cheek. "You do, too, Mama."

Leah used her finger to get the frosting off her face and tasted it. "Perfect." She rubbed noses with Micah. "Thanks for the sample."

December 7

Dear Lucy and Micah,
Today's the day! It's time to deliver the pictures and cookies to our neighbors. I want to make sure we take some to Mr. Johnson next door. Who else do you think we can take deliver to?
Love,
Mama

"Can I knock, Mama?"

When Leah nodded, she handed Lucy one of her plates of cookies and watched Lucy rap her knuckles on the blue door in front of them. She stepped back as it started to open.

"Oh, hello there, Bowers family."

"Hi, Mr. Johnson. We brought you some cookies." Lucy held out the plate.

"That's thoughtful of you, thank you." He peeked at the cookies. "Are those sugar cookies?"

"Yep!" piped up Micah. "Daddy's favorite!"

"Well, that is pretty great."

"They taste *awesome*, too." Micah tugged on Leah's arm. When she leaned down, he whispered, "Can I go to Miss Carol's now?"

Leah nodded and whispered back, "Yes, have Lucy go with you."

Micah grabbed Lucy's hand and pulled. "Lucy! Come with me to Miss Carol's house. Pleeeease."

Lucy followed him, and Leah turned to Mr. Johnson. "How are you?"

"It's weird not having Dad around this year, but I'm doing okay." He cocked his head to the side. "What about you?"

Leah imagined the smile she gave him didn't quite meet her eyes. "I'm managing. Some days are harder than others." She sighed and eyed her children talking to Miss Carol next door. "Trying to bring him into the things we're doing for others this month, hoping it helps them remember him."

Mr. Johnson nodded. "What a good idea for keeping his memory alive during the holidays." He watched the kids, who were laughing with Miss Carol. "It seems like they're doing okay today."

"Today's a good day. They've had some giggles."

"You're doing a good job, Leah. You probably don't hear that enough now."

She swallowed a sob. "Thank you." She offered him a hug. "We'll see you later. We have a couple more houses to get to."

December 10

Dear Lucy and Micah,
One of Daddy's favorite things for us to do was ride around and look at lights. Today, we'll decorate our outside trees and the windows for other people to see our lights.
Love,
Mama

"How's this look, Mama?" Lucy held a wreath up in the kitchen window.
"I like it!" Leah helped her hang it before walking outside with Micah.
"Mama?"
"Hmm?"
"Can we put lights on the fence, too?"
Micah's face held hope, and Leah couldn't resist. "We can try. I think some of the clips we bought will work for that." She mussed his hair. "We'll find out together."
"Mama?"
"Yes?"
"What do you get when you cross a snowman with a vampire?"
"Umm . . . I don't know."
"Frostbite." Micah burst into giggles.

December 15

Dear Lucy and Micah,
The house looks beautiful. You've worked so hard to get it ready for the holidays this year. Today, you're spending time with Aunt Teresa, Aunt Darla, and Uncle Jon. Sometimes the greatest gift we can give is listening. I hope that, today, you will ask your aunts and uncle about what your daddy was like growing up. And then listen.
Love,
Mama

Lucy and Micah were laughing as they climbed into the car. "It sounds like you had a good time today."

"Did you know that Daddy used to beg Grandma to make sugar cookies every year at this time?" asked Lucy, her blonde ponytail bouncing.

"Yeah," continued Micah, "but Aunt Teresa said Grandma wasn't a very good baker, so every year, they were either burnt or yucky to eat."

Leah found herself giggling with her children. "I didn't know that, but I bet that's why he was always wanting to eat the frosting and not wait for cookies."

Lucy's jaw dropped. "I bet you're right, Mama."

"Daddy also used to cheat anytime he played games with Uncle Jon," snickered Micah.

"Like someone else I know," mumbled Lucy.

"I do not cheat!" hollered Micah.

"How do you know I was talking about you then?"

Micah slumped against his seat and folded his arms across his chest. "Whatever."

"Okay, you two." Leah shook her head. "He told me about that. Uncle Jon almost always set up games in his favor, drawing from the bottom of card piles or dealing himself the best cards."

"Like Lucy," whispered Micah.

"Micah." Leah's voice held a warning.

"Uncle Jon told us that part, too." Lucy frowned. "He said at first he did it to be funny cause Daddy would get mad, but he stopped when he realized Daddy was *really* angry. But Daddy didn't stop when Uncle Jon did. Uncle Jon let him do it anyway."

"Aunt Darla said she used to dress Daddy up like her doll," giggled Micah from the backseat, his hands covering his mouth.

"She said he wasn't a very pretty girl," added Lucy.

Leah smirked. "I can imagine he wasn't."

December 18

Dear Lucy and Micah,
Today, I want you each to invite someone over for Daddy's favorite meal. You should choose someone who doesn't have someone else to have dinner with tonight. You'll help me make dinner.

Love,
Mama

"Mama! Do we *have* to have shepherd's pie for dinner?" Lucy's face was full of disgust. "I mean, really?!"

"What?" yelled Micah. "I hate shepherd's pie."

Leah reassured her children. "No, we're not making shepherd's pie."

"I thought we were making Daddy's favorite?" Lucy's face twisted in confusion.

"Well, my loves, Daddy *did* like shepherd's pie, but it wasn't his favorite. His favorite was chicken fajitas with mango pineapple salsa."

"Oh." Micah nodded. "I'll eat those."

"Me too."

"Shepherd's pie was his favorite when he was a kid, and he really wanted you to try it. He hoped you'd love it, too, but it's okay that you don't."

Lucy shook her head and stuck out her tongue. "Good thing, because blech."

"Who should we invite?" wondered Leah.

"What about Mr. Dale? Miss Peggy died so he doesn't have anyone at home now."

"Good idea, Micah. I like that."

"What about Miss Marge? Her kids live far away, so she's in her big house all by herself."

"Great choice, Lucy. I'll call them later. For now, you two can cut some peppers and onions. I'll cut some chicken and marinade it."

"Onions? Are they gonna make me cry?"

"I don't know, sis, they might. Sometimes onions do that when you cut them." Leah reached into the cabinet and pulled out three cutting boards. "Did you know that this meal is the first thing your Daddy ever made for me?"

Micah's chocolate-brown eyes stared up at her. His appearance was so much like his daddy that it took her breath away. She slid a finger across her cheek.

"Maybe that's why I like it so much," said Lucy, slipping her arm around Leah. "I think this is my favorite thing that Daddy made. I'm glad we're sharing it for dinner tonight."

December 21

Dear Lucy and Micah,
It snowed last night! Today, we're going to take Daddy's snowblower to take care of Miss Carol's and Mr. Johnson's sidewalks for them. Daddy

always helped Miss Carol after her husband passed, and Mr. Johnson usually uses a shovel. Then we'll come home, make snow angels, and have hot chocolate.

Love,
Mama

Their faces were flushed as they stripped out of their wet clothes. "Go grab some blankets, I'll make the hot chocolate." Leah hurried to the kitchen and put some milk on the stove to heat.

"That was. So. Much. Fun!" Micah's eyes shone with joy as he and Lucy joined their mom.

"Yes!" agreed Lucy. She paused. "I wish Daddy was here to do it with us."

Leah knelt beside them and wrapped her arms around them. "Me too, sweetheart."

"He loved to make snow angels." Lucy sobbed in her mom's shoulder.

"No, he didn't," cried Micah.

"Yes, he did!"

"No, he didn't. He liked for *us* to make snow angels." Micah wrapped his blanket tight around him and plopped in a chair.

"He helped us make snowmen," pouted Lucy.

"And he threw snowballs at us," added Micah. "But not hard."

Lucy sunk into a chair. "I miss him."

"Me too."

"Me three." Leah hugged Lucy and Micah, grateful her children were sharing.

December 25

Dear Lucy and Micah,
It's the last day we celebrate this month, although I do hope you find kind things to do for people year-round. Today, we head to the movies, as usual on this day. This time, however, I would like for you to watch the people behind us while we wait in line. Each of you pick one person who looks like they came alone, and we will pay for their ticket. Hopefully, they feel loved today. I'm so proud of both of you, and I love you very much.

Love,
Mama

Lucy and Micah bounced on their toes as they waited in line, looking behind them for someone to give free tickets. Leah peered at the matinee to see what was playing. They usually saw the new family movie, but the theater had started something new this year and were showing a different "oldie" every day.

"Hey, kids." She waved her hand behind her to get their attention while she focused on the movies that were playing. "Guys?" She reached back again but didn't find them. "Lucy? Micah?" She turned around and gasped. Her hand went to her chest, and she rubbed the necklace she was wearing.

"Mama! Look who I found!" Lucy held tightly to Miss Carol's hand, pulling her along.

"Hi, Carol." Leah reached for the older woman and embraced her. When they stepped back, Leah noticed the tears in her eyes and nodded in understanding. She squeezed her hand. "Please let us pay for your ticket today."

"Hey, Mommy! I found Mr. Dale!" Micah came running to her, then stopped to turn around and run back to the retired minister. "Come on," he stage-whispered. "It's okay, really!"

As they approached, Leah reached out and gave Dale a hug. "It's nice to see you today."

"Thank you, it's nice to see you three, too." He studied the line he had surpassed. "I just needed to be around people today."

"No need to explain, my friend." Leah indicated the woman next to her. "This is my neighbor and friend, Carol. Carol, this is my friend, Dale."

The two shook hands before returning their gaze to Leah. "Do you know what you want to see?" asked Leah. "We usually do the newest family movie, but I saw the 'oldie' they're offering. It was Jacob's favorite, so I thought we might watch it instead." She turned to the kids, who had high-fived each other. "I take it that's okay?"

"Yes!" they exclaimed.

Carol smiled sadly. "That was my Robert's favorite, too." Her head dropped. "It's the reason I came today. It's kind of like he's here with me."

"It's not really my favorite," said Dale, "but Jacob introduced me to it a few years ago. I could see it again."

"You don't have to see that. We'll still pay for your ticket."

"I didn't have a definite plan for what I was going to see. Like I said, I just needed to be around people today."

"Will you sit with us?" asked Micah. Leah observed his interaction with Dale, noting to herself that a month ago, he would barely talk to anyone besides her.

"Certainly, young Micah." Dale smiled at the young man beside him. "I'll even tell you, 'You'll shoot your eye out, kid!' if you want."

The others laughed. Lucy continued to hold Miss Carol's hand, like she was afraid her neighbor would scurry away from them if she let go.

Leah paid for their tickets, and they started toward the usher taking the tickets. She slowed and considered the group chattering. *An odd mix*, she thought, *but brought together in our grief*. She thought of Jacob, wishing again that he was still with them, saddened that he'd no longer be with them for special occasions, or even every day. It was in the everyday things that she missed him most.

"Mama?" Leah blinked when she felt Lucy's hand in hers. "Mama?"

"Yes, my little love?"

Lucy hugged her mom and looked up at her. "I know Daddy isn't here anymore, but this month, with the things you had us do? Things that were his favorite, things he liked to do? It was kind of like he was with us again, home for the holidays, you know?"

About the Author

Melissa Cate has always been a storyteller—when she was a preschooler, her mom would record the bedtime stories Melissa would tell at night and type them up for her. After thirty years of mostly academic, devotional, or biographical writing, she jumped headfirst back into fiction in October 2023 and was a Write on the River winner in the spring of 2024. She has published four short stories in anthologies in 2025, and her first novel is planned to be published in 2026. Melissa currently lives in the Pacific Northwest with her family but is a Midwesterner through and through.

You can find Melissa on Instagram:
@melissacatewrites

To learn more about Melissa, visit her website at:
https://www.melissacate.com

Farolito

Farolito

yesenia monique

Time has an uncanny way of sliding faster toward Winter every year. I imagine the seasons as a wheel, each with their equally sized wedges fitted together, yet somehow January seems to stretch its wintry limbs far longer than any other. Life, death, and rebirth is the endless cycle that consumes everything within our bubble, perfectly contained within a vast expanse of darkness. Within that darkness, however, are tiny speckles of mesmerizing light along our path. One of these is my abuela, like a *farolito*[1] herself, a magical burning flame that guides our spirits back to family. What do we do, though, when our own flames are teetering upon extinction?

I stare at the big, bold capital letter *W*, and my heart sinks as the feeling of forlorn dread begins to set in again.

It's the third year in a row, I angrily remind myself, keeping my eyes glued to the calendar date on my phone. I can feel the heat rising to my head as the blood begins to boil over, ruining the peaceful lull I had been enjoying. My racing heartbeat obscures the festive music I have playing in the background.

Deep breaths, I quickly remind myself and close my eyes. I have to keep calm. Otherwise they win. I imagine this as a game for some corporate pomp who sits

---

[1] *farolito*: a type of holiday lantern.

slackly behind a black, flat computer monitor, grinning deviously as they assign overtime shifts for each firefighter. Their cruel sense of humor squealing its way in as they enter those pesky forced-hire dates that result in 48- or 72-hour shifts, annoyingly and exhaustingly more tedious than the usual 24.

Of course Ethan would be working.

The rising smell of burning eggs encircles my nostrils, making my eyes shoot open to the pan my mind has recklessly abandoned on the stove burner. The caked-in, browning mess will take forever to scrub off.

Better to just toss the whole thing in the trash. I feel the bitterness lingering in the recesses of my thoughts as I turn the nob with my free hand, my screen, still lit with the calendar view, in the other.

Rolling my eyes, I abandon my phone on the counter and run my fingers comfortingly through my hair. I move through the curly mess, slowly massaging my roots. This is not how I imagined my life would be. Every day I feel myself falling further into a lonely abyss, everyone around me receding into the background of a once vibrant life: friends; family; and a partner who feels unreachable for long, agonizing stretches of time. I hate his job; Ethan knows it even though we rarely talk about it. I know he's doing it for us, for our future, but it still continues to remain the giant elephant that sits in every corner of our world.

As if the universe can sense my debilitating anguish, the familiar slow drumming of the conga gently winds its way through the speaker, softly prickling my ears. I begin to ease a bit, anticipating the sweet, wistful strumming of the acoustic guitar that always transports me to the kitchen of my childhood home. Slowly, poco á poco, resurfacing the enlivening memory.

There I am, steadily swaying my body to the Caribbean rhythm. Like the bright *farolito* lanterns, my soul begins to soar up into the night sky. I catch the blissful melody that rises through my abuela's vocal cords. Notes full of joy. I can feel my own heart singing in perfect synchronicity with Gloria Estefan. In this moment, the three of us—Gloria, my grandmother, and me—feel the magic of our favorite season budding, flowering as it carefully curves around and envelops our enchanted spirits. Enriched with love and hope, we are ready to celebrate our upcoming *Noche Buena*.[2]

I'm not ready to let go of the dance, but my mind spins me off into my abuela's downstairs basement, where my cousin and I are having our traditional holiday movie marathon.

"You know what I'm craving?" my cousin asks, lifting an eyebrow as we leisurely sit on the oversized floral sofa chair.

---

[2] *Noche Buena:* December holiday traditions culminating into a night of music and dancing.

"I can hear the blender from here!" I squeal, and we shoot up, racing toward the narrow staircase, the old wood creaking tiredly beneath our feet.

Back in the kitchen, the familiar music excites our spirits the same way the euphoric smells of sacred family recipes rouse our taste buds. In the oven, the sweet, powdery textures of the flaky guava pastries make our mouths water as we hold the creamy cinnamon and coconut notes of *coquito*[3] in our cocktail glasses. These are the staples no member of our family can do without. Virgin for the kids and a splash of Bacardi for the adults. Beginning the first day of December, *coquito* is consistently on tap, expected and available without pause.

The fridge is well stocked at all times, because once sunset comes around, we never know when the percussions are going to come knocking.

"*Saludo! Saludo! Vengo á saludar!*" the late-night visitors sing, bringing the season's greetings. Clamoring loudly with tambourines, maracas, güiros, and trumpets while our city block sleeps.

"*Uno, dos, tres, habre la puerta ya!*" The chorus repeats until the little row house lights up like the living room evergreen. Our tired eyes are replaced with exhilaration as we welcome, feast, and dance with our guests. A living room dance party booms through the night as my cousin and I lock hands with our abuela, circling and singing together in the small space. When the time is right, the adults deliberate where to take the *trulla*[4] next. Which unsuspecting family is about to be jolted from their slumber?

December always had a sense of magical rhythm to it. It was easy to see why this time of year was my abuela's favorite. A little piece of the island, her original home, pulsing through our hearts. This was perhaps why, after her death during the very season that invigorated her, the resulting rupture could never fully heal. We tried to re-create the spark year after year, but it seemed she was the one glue that could hold us all together.

As the usual problem solver that I am, I pick up my phone from the counter and scroll through my contacts until I land on Gigi's number. Maybe this could be the year my cousin and I finally rekindle the charm within our relatives.

"I can't host, Mari. We'll still be unpacking and organizing the house from the move. Have you talked to tia Iselda?" asked Gigi. At the sound of her voice,

---

[3] *coquito:* a creamy, coconut-based, Puerto Rican beverage that is a staple in holiday celebrations.

[4] *trulla:* a group of people who go from house to house singing holiday songs.

I could still picture our matching foam 'staches from the *coquito* we had just raided from the kitchen. Laughing and drinking until our bellies ached.

"She's going out of town this year. She's repeatedly mentioned wanting to spend the holidays on some cruise deck," I say, slumping into my table chair.

Tia Iselda had hosted a few times, but the family usually scattered to different corners of the city by nightfall. No *trulla* ever came knocking. I couldn't blame Gigi for not wanting to host, not wanting the letdown of unanswered invitations and the gut-wrenching disappointment of a faraway dream.

"I'm sorry, really. But you know . . . I don't think anyone is interested anymore." Her tone seems strained, and I can tell she's already moved on. "Say hi to *titi* for me?"

"Of course," I say. As the call disconnects, I decide to look up flight schedules to my parents'. It might still be early enough to get a good price on tickets. I just wish Ethan were joining me. For the second year in a row, I'll be spending the holidays in a town nowhere near my abuela.

"You're leaving again this year?" Ethan's frown makes me surprisingly more angry than sympathetic. He just got home after his twenty-four-hour shift, and we're already pouncing on each other.

"Have you looked at the calendar? You're working an assigned-hire code *and* a regular shift segment the whole week of the twentieth!"

This means that he would work every other day and one forty-eight-hour shift before his three-day break. He'll miss Mother's Night, Solstice, and *Noche Buena* this time around. Our partnership feels like it's ripping apart during what's supposed to be the most magical time of the year—a common theme for many firefighter families. I imagine the corporate pomp rolling on the floor in laughter now.

"Really?" He sighs, pulling out his phone for confirmation. I still can't believe he doesn't check our shared calendar as frequently as I do, but then again, I have always been the planner, constantly one jump and two steps ahead. "Yup . . . wow, that's a bummer," he says, his hand to his chin as casually as if his fantasy football league had lost another game.

My wide-eyed stare and exaggerated pursed lips cause him to pause like a deer in the headlights. "And that's why I'm leaving. AGAIN!"

"Okay, okay. I can see why you're upset." He steps forward and stretches his arms out, inviting me toward him. I hate the way he's always trying to diffuse my anger with a hug, as if the heat would just dissipate within his embrace. "If you stay, I heard the fire house is bringing in a catering company on the twenty-fifth, and a lot of the guys will have their families coming over." His hands are gently rubbing my back, trying to work out my knotted tension.

"I don't know, I'll think about it. My parents will be upset about me not seeing them," I say, feeling lighter under his touch. I pull away enough to look up at his soft expression.

"It'll be a change of scenery. And who knows? Maybe you'll find that magic spark you're constantly running after at the station. You know I'll do anything to make you happy, Mari." His smile is hopeful and reassuring. And he's right about one thing. I'm always running after something; the magic of yesterday eludes me, just out of reach, floating further and further into space like a fading *farolito* in the night sky.

"I'll talk to my parents," I reassure him. My heart is aching, but maybe this is what we need to recapture our own fire. And it's about time I embrace reality.

"Amari!" my mother exclaims, preferring to use my whole name when she's slightly disappointed. "We haven't seen you at all this year," she complains.

"I know, I'm sorry. It's just that I feel bad for Ethan. Having no one to come back to when he *is* home during the holidays."

I felt a little selfish leaving him last year, and a part of me wants to stay home anyway. Spending the nights within my own sanctuary, embracing the solitude instead of pasting on a smile that never fully meets my eyes.

"He really can't come? Can't he trade shifts or something?" I hear her tinkering around in her kitchen, a habit picked up from her mother, my abuela.

"There's no way anyone would trade shifts that week; everyone wants to be partying with their own families. I'll see if I can come up after New Years." I already know Ethan will be working, but I open the calendar app anyway.

"Say hi to Ethan for us, and remind him that he hasn't been over to see us in a while either!"

I roll my eyes. Traveling with him is like playing a game of chess. Making calculated moves just to trade shifts with his coworkers.

Ethan finds me still sitting at the table with my head resting in between my hands, the airline search is still queued up on my I-pad after the phone call with my mom.

"Are you buying flight tickets?" he asks quizzically, his voice is low and slightly dejected.

"Maybe. After New Year's? I figure I should still make a plan to see them.

You're working anyway, so I figure you wouldn't miss me as much." I look up and follow his gaze as he takes a seat opposite me.

"I mean, I always miss you. But if this is what you need to do then I understand."

His softness elicits a small smile from me that barely moves my cheeks. I refrain from bringing up his job. Same story, different day. It'll only sour the mood further, and I've already met my quota of disappointments for the day.

"Thank you, it means a lot."

I dutifully prep my *coquito* and struggle to fight off the pull toward darkness. As the Northern Hemisphere continues its descent into hibernation, as the anniversary of my abuela's death inches nearer, I feel myself wanting to curl inward. Everything about December is meant to lift our spirits: the dazzling lights exist to remind us that the long nights are slowly getting shorter, the vigorous evergreen is meant to keep our memory of nature alive, and the hope for togetherness reminds us to find each other within each passing storm. Yet, my own storm is brewing, and my comforting flames are flickering.

Staring at the blended concoction, making sure the hue is just right, I hear my abuela's comforting words as she makes one of her famous batches in my favorite kitchen:

"Remember that the coconut is the lifeline of *coquito*; it's rich creaminess ties back to the beating heart of the island. The cinnamon is the sprinkle of the earth, our *tierra*, and last but not least . . ." She pauses while taking out a little glass jar filled with seeded stars. "The anise. Every family has their secret recipe; this is what makes ours so special." Her eyes are locked onto the bottle as if she's reliving a memory. Was she, in that moment, leaving her own little kitchen for a faraway dream?

I resolve to make this year's time of *Noche Buena* one of cozy comforts. The staples of *coquito*, guava pastries, and *pernil*[5] will become my comfort foods as I veg on my couch with remote in hand and holiday favorites on full display. I make a convincing argument to myself that this time of quiet solitude may just be the best tradition yet, though my soul doesn't fully buy in.

Mother's Night arrives to kick off my hygge marathon, and I'm already sitting by the fireplace in my pajamas as I light the blood-orange candle. I don't need to pull out the paper with the familiar poem since my mind committed it to memory years ago. As I begin reciting, I let my eyelids fall:

---

[5] *pernil:* a slow-roasted pork shoulder or leg that is a staple in Puerto Rican, Dominican, and Cuban cuisine.

*I call upon my ancestral mothers on this night, I seek your guidance and
your light.*
*I light this candle to honor you, your flame reminds me that from the
darkness we emerge anew.*
*I honor the mothers of blood, spirit, and bone, for your gift of creation I
invite you home.*

My eyes are still closed as I feel a slight breeze on my skin. On this night especially, I think of my abuela and honor the legacy she's left behind. I think of
my own mother, too, and how I might one day join the long line of matriarchs
within my family tree.

The longing desire to carry on our traditions causes me to hear phantom
voices singing, *Saludo, Saludo, vengo á saludar!* A song I yearn to hear again, if
only for just one night. The trumpet cuts in, louder now, crafting the words
with each consecutive note. The bells of the tambourine join in, tapping in syn-
chrony with its partner. Even louder now, the song threatens to knock down my
wooden door. I open my eyes and they're still there, asking to enter.

It can't be . . .

I scramble to get up and run to the door with the kind of smile I haven't
felt in weeks—there's only one person I know who plays the trumpet like that!
On the other side of the door, my late-night visitors are illuminated by the little
amber porchlight: my mother and father are performing a little *parranda*[6] just
for me! I let the tears envelop me as my mother pulls me into a tight embrace,
tambourine clinking against my back.

"How are you here?" I manage to ask, pulling away to see their grinning
faces.

"Ethan," my dad replies. "He arranged the flights to surprise you." My sweet
Ethan gifting me with this little piece of magic he knew I needed. He's trying,
doing the best he can. Even though he's not here, the thoughtfulness isn't lost
on me.

We spend the evening dancing in my little kitchen while we fill our bellies
with powdered pastries and cookies. Moving my body like this is part of the
medicine my soul yearns for, a tiny spec of light in my dark skies. The three of us
make plans to bake sun bread, a favorite Solstice tradition, and talk about how
visiting the fire station is an exciting, new activity we've never even considered.
Ethan has apparently promised my father that he'll take us on the engine for a
quick ride, sirens and all wailing through the streets. For the first time since he
started with the department, I'm realizing his job can have its perks.

---

[6] *parranda:* a lively holiday tradition where friends and family gather to sing traditional
carols, visiting homes often unannounced, late into the night.

"Is it okay to bring some *pastelillos*[7] and *coquito* to share? I know there's catered food, but I'd like to share a bit of our *Noche Buena* staples, too," I ask Ethan on one of the nights he's home.

"Yes! I don't think anyone would turn down extra desserts, and Cap will definitely welcome all of it." His work family consists of eight other firefighters and two captains. Some would have their parents, siblings, nieces and nephews visiting. It's shaping up to be quite a party.

"You know what we should do? Bring a small *parranda* to the station! I bet the kids would love it," my dad says, his eyes lighting up as he picks up a stray maraca and shakes it."

"There you go! That's a great idea!" My mom joins in, clapping her hands together in a similar beat.

I let out a "*Wepa!*[8]" and catch Ethan staring at me with a huge smile.

"I'll bring my guitar!" he chimes in.

On the evening of the twenty-fifth, my parents and I pack into my car armed with a trumpet, tambourine, maracas, and a guitar. I make a plan to text Ethan our ETA so he can come out and join us when we get there. A grand musical entrance with my entourage; my abuela would be proud—our *trulla* sharing a little piece of our Caribbean flair.

No one expected our booming entrance, but every face delights in the spectacle. Kids start locking hands and twirling together, while the adults bob their heads in tempo. The firehouse kitchen is abuzz with music and laughter until we finish our set.

"So I heard you brought *coquito*," says Marco, one of Ethan's coworkers. "I actually have a bottle myself. Care to try some?" His lifted eyebrows tell me that he's eager to compare.

"Let's have it!" I respond, and he pours each of us a glass. As the creamy liquid fills the bottom, my mouth salivates in anticipation.

"Cheers!" he says, raising his glass.

"*Buen provecho!*" I reply, letting our glasses clink.

There's a stronger blend of cinnamon and licorice in his version, one that brings me back to the first time I was put in charge of adding the star-shaped

---

[7] *pastelillos de guayaba:* baked puff pastries filled with guava and sprinkled with powdered sugar.

[8] *Wepa:* a versatile slang interjection used to express excitement, joy, or enthusiasm. Akin to "Woohoo!"

anise seed to the simmering liquid on the stove of the little row-house kitchen. Abuela had explained each element of the recipe before taking out one of the stars and handing me the little glass jar. I held it to my nose, letting the spicy-sweet aroma captivate my senses, the warm, woody undertones reminding me of the kindled logs by the make-shift chimney.

"It's this little star that creates the perfect balance of taste in our *coquito*," she said as she lifted the single anise toward the sky. With a look of wonder, she rotated it between her fingers before handing it to me. "Remember to always let this be your North Star, your little piece of paradise no matter where you are."

The memory of her words adds another spec of light within my sky. It's funny the way a familiar scent can transport the mind back to a moment frozen in time, a flawless version of a mystical season, if such a thing as perfect ever did exist. Tonight, this serendipitous gathering at the fire station has made me realize what my abuela knew all along: That the magic we experience isn't bound to one place, event, or circumstance. It is our North Star that grounds us while we navigate the uncharted path. The magic of the past, the present, and the future exists on a timeless scale, looping and intertwining between moments of happenstance, while our star remains the constant. We share traditions and create new ones with relatives, friends, and strangers, and each memory ignites a new, mesmerizing flame along our path, like the *farolitos* guiding our spirits ever forward to a different type of "home."

About the Author

yesenia monique is a designer and storyteller who creatively weaves letterforms together to craft messages that move the spirit and challenge the narrative. As an Art History and Design major and former service-woman, she uses her experiences and cultural education to lift silent voices and deliver unique storylines. Her complex background informs her work as she seeks to highlight marginalized communities.

Her short story "A Killer Dream" appeared in And You Press's *Not As It Seems: A Gothic Anthology*.

She currently resides in Southern California and enjoys being a mother of two, throwing kitchen dance parties, and cozying up with a warm cup of coffee and a good book.

You can find yesenia on Instagram:
@ym.narrative

To learn more about yesenia, visit her website at:
https://www.yeseniamonique.design

I'll Be Anywhere but Home for Christmas

I'll Be Anywhere but Home for Christmas

Morgan Matlow

December 20—Brussels, Belgium

The vendor places the waffle dough onto the hot iron, and it sizzles appreciatively. Under a thick panel of glass, all the waffle options stare back at me: red strawberries and cookie butter, hazelnut spread and banana, heaps of ice cream and sprinkles, among other tremendous amounts of sugary delectables that would rot right through my teeth.

Hattie would love this. She'd probably pick the banana one, drawn in by the idea of European Nutella melting on the hot, freshly made waffle. She'd probably insist that the vendor add extra hazelnut spread.

The man next to me gets ready to place an order with the vendor while I continue to stare at the options, unsure of which choice to make. Hattie would have helped me. She would have told me to get the strawberry one. But that feels too simple. I'm in Brussels. This should be an adventure. So, while my tastebuds draw me to the one that feels safe, the choice isn't that simple.

"One with hazelnut spread and strawberry, please," the man says in an American accent.

Coming on this trip, I thought I was leaving all my cares behind, throwing myself into a whole new world. Hattie, who? I was supposed to be engulfed in hot, European men, men who could distract me from remembering how much James hurt me when he started dating Hattie; maybe one of them could even make me forget Hattie's part in the betrayal. Instead, everywhere I turn are throngs of American tourists, reminding me that I have not taken on an exotic, new European life, but instead am one of a million cattle fighting over something the locals would never consume.

The American man pulls back from the counter and stands beside me. "What did you get?" he asks. He's casual in his delivery, like he's already pegged me as an English speaker. I wonder what it is about me that's so obviously American. He, in turn, looks like he could be most anything, wrapped in a sleek black winter coat, red scarf draped over his shoulders, his dark curls just long enough to graze the scarf at the nape of his neck.

I cross my arms in a defensive pose. "I haven't chosen yet." My gaze connects with his hazel one, and I peel my glance away.

"The banana looks good," he says.

"Well, why didn't you get that one, then?"

"I did a mixture. The Nutella with strawberries."

"That's almost too simple."

"These waffles aren't like the American ones. They have pearl sugar in them, so any of these extreme toppings . . ." He motions to one with a heaping of marshmallows and M&Ms on it. "Will overwhelm the natural flavor of the waffle."

He's probably right.

I step up to the counter and order the cookie butter, or *speculoos*, they call it, and strawberry.

When I walk back to wait near him, he smirks at me, the background of twinkling lights and red ribbons making him look almost magical.

"I'm Kara," I say, reaching a gloved hand out for him to shake.

He grabs my hand. "Carter."

Our waffles are finished at about the same time, and they come with teeny, little plastic forks to eat them.

"Mind if I join you?" Carter asks, following me to a corner near the Manneken Pis, a famous statue of a little boy peeing. They've draped twinkle lights around him and wrapped a scarf around his neck, making a perfect place for me to sit and eat my waffle.

"Sure," I say, cutting a small piece off the waffle and taking a bite. It's caramelized around the edges from the melted pearl sugar, and absolutely heavenly. "You were right about this. It's amazing."

He takes a bite of his own waffle. He opens his mouth to say something, but quickly changes his mind, leaving us both to eat in silence. Not complete silence, as somewhere in the middle of the market, Christmas carols play.

"It's got to be in here somewhere!" Hattie flipped through the pages of her Christmas songbook as quickly as her stubby little nine-year-old fingers would let her.

The treehouse was lit by an old string of red and green Christmas lights Mom and Dad had wanted to throw out. Every fifth or sixth light had burned out, leaving a weird gap in the lighting. Small tufts of snow made their way into the treehouse through the gaps in the wood, but we'd planned for this, placing a sleeping bag on the ground to protect our butts from the snow.

"I can just pick a song," I said, reaching for the book, but she ripped it from me.

"No! It's my turn to pick, and I thought of the perfect one." She flipped harder before her eyes landed on the prize. She turned to the CD player beside her, skipping to track number 10. The song began to play a recognizable tune.

I nestled in next to my sister and handed her a mug of the steaming cocoa I'd made for us. Then we sang. We were offkey for half of it, and Hattie couldn't for the life of her hit the high note. When we finished, we held each other's hands, closed our eyes, and spoke our Christmas wishes aloud. We'd done this same thing every year on Christmas Eve since we were seven, snuck out of our beds and into the treehouse, making it back just in time to be in bed before eleven. That way we could be asleep before midnight, so Santa could come. We'd hope each year that he'd bring us our Christmas wish.

When we finish our waffles, I finally say, "What brings you to Brussels to eat a tourist waffle all by yourself?"

He looks at his feet, avoiding eye contact with me. "My wife died last year. We had this trip booked. I couldn't really cancel. It felt like canceling a date with her. I know, it sounds weird."

Great, I just ate my tourist waffle with a man on a date with his dead wife. How romantic. "I'm sorry for your loss," I manage to say.

"What brings *you* here by yourself?" he asks.

The first rule of being a woman traveling alone is to never admit that you're traveling alone. "I'm here with my sister," I say.

"And she let you come downtown in Brussels at night all by yourself to get a waffle?"

"She wasn't feeling well." I eye him. Just because he's a widower doesn't mean that he's safe. For all I know, he killed his wife.

"Sorry," he says. "That probably sounded like I'm someone you don't want to be caught alone with at night in Brussels. And just for that, I'm going to back away now, and say goodnight."

"Goodnight," I say, nodding my head at him in understanding. Though

I should have been turned off by the way he asked if I was alone, I still somehow felt safe with him. And, as he disappears into the crowd of people jostling around each other with bags in hand, I can't help but think of James.

"I've met someone else," James said. He'd been late to meet me for a Pilates class we were supposed to go to that day.

The news hits my chest like a boulder. I hadn't anticipated this. I'd thought things were going in the opposite direction. He was supposed to propose. Not break up with me.

"Who?" was the only word I found myself able to say. I wanted to ask why. I wanted to ask what was so wrong with me. I wanted to ask when things had changed. But all I could ask was who. As if that mattered more than anything else.

"Hattie," he said.

And that was the moment I began plotting my revenge against Hattie Elaine Rothchild.

December 21—Valkenburg, Netherlands

When I thought of a Christmas market tour through Europe, I never pictured rain. I pictured snowcapped roofs and dazzling Christmas lights reflecting off the ice on the ground. But today has not been snowy. The day only comes with rain. My puffer jacket doesn't do much to keep the rain off me, especially since today's is more of a mist than a downfall. I'm going to get wet no matter how I cover my face.

Hattie probably knew Dutch winters come with more rain than snow. She probably would have put "rain jacket" on our packing list. She would have looked at the weather days ahead of time and already made plans for us.

It's the fourth day of my Christmas-market adventure for one. Valkenburg is the third city of five in Europe that Hattie and I had planned to experience together. Back when she was still my best friend and not just my traitorous sister.

"Kara, do you see how magical it would be?" Hattie asked, pulling up picture after picture from her Pinterest board. "The food. The atmosphere. The men."

"Men for you. Not for me," I said, remembering the ring box I'd seen in James's dresser when I'd fetched him a pair of socks one day.

"Don't remind me. I'll probably never have my sister again. You'll always be attached to this man, all girlhood extinguished."

"Girlhood extinguished? You realize you're twenty-five, right?"

"Yes. Don't you see? This trip would be the pinnacle of our girlhood. Every Christmas memory wrapped up into one beautiful adventure. But you're saying no to me because you want to save for a wedding when James hasn't even proposed."

"We can go one day, Hattie. But just not right now."

I'd been both right and wrong to not plan the trip with her then. It turns out I didn't need the money for a wedding after all, but I also didn't need her to go with me.

After James broke up with me, I gave Hattie the opposite of everything I gave James. I yelled and fought with him, called him every name in the book. Hattie, who hurt me more than James ever could, I gave the silent treatment. I haven't even talked to her since before the breakup.

I did see Hattie once. I was shopping for Thanksgiving. I was on my own this year, because I couldn't stand the chance of seeing her and James at Thanksgiving with Mom and Dad. They'd picked Hattie's side in all of this, telling me that blood was thicker than water. That my sister was my sister, no matter who she'd fallen in love with.

She and James stood in the cereal aisle, picking out what they'd be eating after sleeping over at Mom and Dad's house, I guessed. I watched them for a moment. She'd snuggled herself into his arms, and they gazed at the cereal like it was the most delicious thing they'd ever seen. They didn't see me, and I ducked out of the way and left the store.

I knew I wouldn't be able to stand Christmas around them; I'd hardly been able to handle two seconds watching them in the grocery store. That's when I booked the trip. I'd be going on the European Christmas market adventure Hattie had talked about for years. And I'd be doing it without her. Over Christmas. Every moment she noticed me missing, she'd remember where I was and what I was doing. And I'd be sending Mom updates.

I take a photo of an old church to send to Mom. There's a huge Christmas tree outside it, decorated with thick, gold ribbons and little lights. I'm sure it would be gorgeous at night.

I make my way across the street to the entrance of my Christmas market of the day and buy myself a ticket for entry.

This market is located in a cave system underground. It's nice to be somewhere dry. I guess even from what Hattie did plan, she did it well. Indoor market for the rainy day.

As I step into the cave, I can practically see her there, shaking off the water from her rain jacket. But she isn't there. It's just me, staring down the Christmas-themed market stalls and Christmas glow of the cave.

I walk among the shops, taking in the bits and bobs each vendor is selling. The scent of chocolate and peppermint floats throughout the cave, getting stronger the deeper into it I walk. A cave might sound like a creepy place to hold a market, but every corner of it is lit by the glimmering Christmas lights. Some green, some red. Some sparkly white, some rainbow. It faintly reminds me of the lights in our treehouse, and the moments Hattie and I used to sit out there, singing carols and making our Christmas wish. Something in me aches for those simpler moments. Something in me wishes Hattie were here to make this moment just as special.

An ornament stall nearby just makes me miss her more, and I step forward reluctantly. We used to go shopping every year for new ornaments to decorate the family tree. Mom would buy each of us just one. When we got old enough to be conscious of it, we'd started picking them out for each other. Then, when we moved out and away from each other, we began buying them for each other's Christmas trees. My eye is drawn to a little reindeer riding in a sleigh. It's the cutest thing, hand carved into wood, with details painted on. Hattie would love it.

A pang in my chest practically pushes me away from the stall, reminding me that Hattie and I don't do that for each other anymore. Our relationship is no longer magical like it once was.

A few steps away, I spot a familiar red scarf in front of a stall selling figurines. Deciding to get my mind off traitorous sisters, I walk toward him.

"Hey," I call out, "Carter."

His head of dark curls turns to look at me, eyebrows curved toward each other in surprise at someone knowing his name. When he sees me, his face brightens, and he puts on a smile.

"Kara, right?" he asks.

I nod. "What brings you here? Not following me, I hope." I put on a cheeky smile of my own, attempting to make it clear that I'm joking.

"It's nice to see you," he says. "And despite how charming I found you the other night, I have not changed my entire European Christmas market plan just to follow you around."

"So, you're on a European Christmas market tour too?" I ask.

"Rochelle, my wife, had it all planned out. I see you're sister-less again today."

"I wasn't completely forthcoming before. I didn't actually come with my sister."

"Ah." He nods in understanding.

"Do you want to get some hot chocolate?" I ask. "The smell is driving me to the weirdest craving."

We walk further into the caves, passing more booths selling candied nuts, stroopwafels covered in chocolate and marshmallows, and even little speculoos cookies shaped like Sinterklaas. But it's not until I spot the hot chocolate stand that my walking speeds up. We get in line, and when it's our turn, Carter doesn't let me pay for my own.

Hot cocoa in hand, I feel ready for conversation again. "So, where are you planning to go next?"

"Tomorrow I'm supposed to be in Germany. Regensberg, I think." He pulls something up on his phone to confirm, then shows me.

"No way! I have one more day here, and then I'm headed there too." I take a sip of the cocoa, letting the warmth of it fill me and enter my soul. It feels like the exact thing I was missing on this cold and rainy day.

"You must think a lot like Rochelle did then," he says, looking at the ground. He's been so nice, but I know there's a part of him that would much rather be here with someone else. I'm starting to relate.

"My sister, Hattie, actually planned the itinerary for this," I say. "I came without her."

"Why would you do that?"

I look down into the swirls rising to the top of my cocoa, then take a sip. "It was my dumb revenge for her hurting me a couple of months ago. I took her itinerary and went on her dream sister trip without her."

"Oh wow," he says thoughtfully. He probably thinks this is some dramatic overreaction. But he doesn't know what she did. And I don't think I could bring myself to tell him. We're silent for a moment again before he says, "Do you want to meet up again in Regensberg? I'll still be there in two days when you get there."

For as little as I've talked to this man, I can sense that he doesn't want to be alone on his trip. It's the same need for companionship I've felt since being here. None of this Christmas magic feels quite magical without someone to share it with.

We walk a little farther, finishing our hot chocolates and making small talk. Carter is from Iowa and has two siblings, both of whom moved a state away when they became adults. His parents passed away when he was twenty-one, and he is now thirty-three. He was married for five years, and then his wife passed away a couple of months ago. I hadn't really been considering Carter as a romantic prospect before, but now I know how fresh his loss is, it's clear that this thing between us is a simple gesture of companionship between two people who've had their lives ripped away from them. Granted, his story is much more dire and heart-wrenching than mine.

As we walk through the stalls a second time, we pass the booth with the Christmas ornaments. The reindeer-on-a-sleigh ornament beckons me back over to it, and Carter notices.

"You should get it," he says, giving me a little nudge.

December 23—Regenburg, Germany

Carter and I meet up again in Regenberg where we sip on mugs of gluhwein. The drink is warm, wrapping me up in the Christmas spirit with spices and sugar accenting the wine and citrus. It's like one of those pots of spices and orange that Hattie used to boil on the stove, sending the scent throughout the entire house. She'd love this.

"Did you come to the market yesterday?" I ask Carter.

"I went to a different one. At a castle. The lady that lives there came out and sang some German Christmas carols. It was really cool. You should check it out tomorrow if you'll still be here."

This market is much more involved than some of the others. It has an ice-skating rink, a Ferris wheel, and sits in the square of a gorgeous cathedral bathed in a deep blue light.

Hattie and I were ten and twelve. I pulled her out onto the ice rink that the local college used for hockey games. And, each year, they decorated it for Christmas season. They pulled out fir trees and Christmas lights, sending the whole rink into the season with the scent of peppermint.

The year prior, Hattie had broken her ankle out on that ice, and she had sworn that she would never return to it, not even for Christmas.

I lured her out anyway, pulling her away from the ten-year-old boy she had been attempting to flirt with.

"Hey," she growled at me.

"Christmas is our thing," I told her. "And so is skating."

"You know why we came. I don't want to skate."

"Well, you put those things on your feet, didn't you?" I gave a pointed look down at the skates on her feet and the heavy wool socks poking out of them.

"Well, I don't want to skate with you. *I was hoping* someone else *would ask me to skate."*

"Hattie. Boys will come and go. You'll probably have forgotten about that guy by New Year's. You and me should be together for all things Christmas. Forever."

Reluctantly, she skated, holding onto my arms for balance, still worried about her ankle. Eventually, she found her skating spark again, laughing and dancing to the music they blasted over the speakers.

She told me later that I was right. That boy had a girlfriend, and she was glad she hadn't wasted the day worrying about him.

We promised each other that we'd always spend Christmas together.

Carter tells me about a Christmas market in Salzburg, Austria, that has a parade of Krampuses each year. The rowdy Krampuses wear full costumes, including masks, with bells that jingle as they run through the streets, smacking revelers on the butts with brooms.

"Rochelle was adamant that we miss that tradition," he says.

It doesn't sound like something Hattie would have liked much either. I laugh. "It sounds kind of fun."

There's a glimmer in his eyes. "Maybe you and I could take a little detour."

The invitation is nice, and the feeling that I don't have to be alone on this trip is inviting. But maybe that's just the gluhwein talking. I don't give a response.

"Or is that something your sister already had planned for you?" he asks.

I look to the ground. "No, Hattie wouldn't have put something like that on the itinerary. There's probably a reason why it's not there."

Carter reaches one hand out, putting it on my shoulder. "It's obvious that you miss her."

I don't want to miss her. But with all the glowing lights and the citrusy flavors in the gluhwein, being reminded of her at every turn, I do. I miss what we were.

"Listen, I don't know why you had to go on this whole Christmas market rampage without her. I'm not sure what she did, but if it's making you miserable to be here without her, maybe it isn't worth it."

I shake my head, trying to keep in the tears that sting at my eyes. "You don't understand." I say the words, not ready to talk about what happened or why it hurt so much.

"I know. But I'm missing someone who should be here, too. I'll never see her again. I can't help but be jealous of you. I know that it's not your romantic partner that you're missing, but I would love to have my Christmas market buddy here. I'm here in memory of her. And it almost seems you're here to overwrite the memory of yours."

"Is it working for you?" I ask.

"I remember Rochelle at every corner."

"And I remember Hattie."

"Look at us, both depressed in one of the most magical places at the most magical time of year."

"I'm sure Rochelle would be happy you still came."

"She would be." We sit in silence for a moment before he says, "For the record, I think Christmas should be spent with the people who make you feel like home. Mine's gone, but I feel her here. I don't think you should run away from that."

His words sit with me through the rest of the night as we walk through the shops. I'm not sure how there could be so many different Christmas-themed items in the world, but each of these markets has had their own unique offerings. New gifts and trinkets and treasures to make me miss Hattie and remind me that Christmas Eve is tomorrow.

It's under the glow of another gigantic Christmas tree, wishing that I wasn't here, but at home, that I make up my mind.

December 24—Home for Christmas

As I climb the ladder to the treehouse, I wonder if Hattie will even be here. I grab at the rungs, which are old and worn, slippery from the ice. But I'm prepared for this. My gloves have grips on them, and I've learned over the years to take it slow as I climb.

What I'm not prepared for is how my heart hammers in my chest. The anxiety builds as I question if this moment will show that Hattie and I keep our promises from all those years ago. She's still blocked on my phone, but my heart isn't completely fossilized. If she's up there, sitting in the treehouse on the sleeping bag, my heart might just begin to heal. If she's holding not one, but two hot chocolates, that would be all I need to bring my Christmas-loving heart back to life.

When I reach the last rung, I inhale deeply. It's the moment of truth.

I pull myself up onto the deck of the treehouse, where I can look directly inside. The Christmas lights are on, strewn around the treehouse like they are every year. But there's no Hattie sitting inside. There's no sleeping bag or cocoa. Instead, thin streaks of snow line the wooden floor.

I'm so stupid. I came all this way home for Christmas Eve, hoping that I could give Hattie one last chance. But her not being here only shows me that she's given up on me. After hurting me so badly when she got together with James, she can't even be here now, when I need her most.

Because that's what hurts, more than anything—Hattie couldn't be there for me when James broke up with me. She couldn't console me and tell me that he was dumb for doing it. And now, all I wanted was some sign that I still matter to her. And that she just might pick me over some dumb boy. But we aren't preteens anymore. We're full-grown women who have our own lives.

And, apparently, Hattie's life doesn't include me.

I sit on the wet, snowy floor, letting the tears stream down my already icy cheeks.

All the pictures I sent Mom of my trip meant nothing to her. My revenge didn't even hurt her for a moment. I'd been so ready to apologize even though *she'd* hurt *me*. I squeeze my eyes closed, wishing that I could be back in Europe, where at least they had gluhwein and German pretzels.

The smell of chocolate and peppermint fills my nose, an unwelcome memory surfacing again. I try to push it down, but the scent only gets stronger. The weight of something soft hits me in the chest. I don't dare to look for a moment, unsure whether these sensations are real.

When I open my eyes, Hattie's bright green eyes stare back at me. Her hair is pulled into messy pigtails, and her eyes are rimmed with red like she's been crying.

"Kara?" Her expression is full of wonder at seeing me. She finishes climbing into the treehouse, thermos of cocoa on her hip. Some cocoa has leaked out onto her candy cane pajama pants.

"Hey, Hattie," I say, my tone low. Just because she's here doesn't mean she wants to make up with me.

"I thought you were still in Europe. Mom said you wouldn't be home until after Christmas."

"I came home early. I wanted to be here." *I wanted to be with you.*

She nods her head slowly, taking it in. I can tell there's a million questions buzzing around in her head, probably just as many as are in mine.

"I tried texting you. I've been trying to apologize," she says.

"I saw you guys in the grocery store one day." I can't even say his name. "And you looked so happy. I didn't know what you might want to say to me, but I couldn't bear to hear it."

She looks down, lids heavy with shame.

"I'm so sorry, Kar. I want you to know that. I was stupid. James convinced me that I was the most special thing in the world, and I believed him. But the last thing I wanted to do was hurt you."

There's a pang in my chest. "You did hurt me, though."

"I didn't want him to break up with you. I'd already decided to cut him out of my life for your sake. But then he broke up with you anyway. He told me it was killing him that he couldn't be with me. And he told me that you understood."

"He's a liar. I never said that."

"I know that now. I realized he lied to me. And I realized that if he did that to you, he could do the same to me. And it wasn't worth chancing that. Not if I had to lose you in the process."

Realization and shock break over me in waves, one after another. "You broke up with him?"

She nods, her eyes glassy with tears. "I'm so sorry. Seeing you in Europe without me on the trip I planned for us made me realize how badly I'd messed up. I didn't want to be with him for Christmas if it meant I couldn't be with my sister. With you."

I pull her into a tight hug, and the thermos sloshes around at the motion, likely leaking more cocoa all over the place. But it doesn't matter because I have my sister. And we both came home to each other for Christmas.

She grips me tight, holding onto me like she never wants to let go.

When I pull away, I say, "For the record, I was planning on forgiving you even if you didn't break up with him. You can be with him if you want. I just want my sister back."

"No." She doesn't explain further, but she doesn't need to, and I feel my heart repairing itself again.

We set up the sleeping bag that she threw on me, even though my pants are soaked from snow and hers from cocoa. We share the thermos as I tell her all about Carter and the Christmas markets. We make plans to go again next year, and I even convince her to go to the Krampus parade in Salzburg.

I give her the ornament I bought for her in Valkenburg, not even knowing if I'd ever see her again. She gives me one that she bought months ago. Hattie lets me choose our Christmas song, and we sing together.

And this year we arrive at the same, shared wish, instantly: to always find our way home for Christmas—the true home that we only find in each other's company.

About the Author

Having channeled her life-long obsession with stories into writing, **Morgan Matlow** has a bachelor's of arts degree in Creative Writing. When not writing, she can be found concocting new recipes, traveling the world, or exploring the mountains near her home in Northern Utah with her husband and dog.

You can find Morgan on Instagram:
@bookdevouree

To learn more about Morgan, visit her website at:
www.morganmatlow.com

Christmas
in the
Woods

Christmas in the Woods

Amy Hepp

August 1998

The sorrowful call of a loon pierced the dark night over the lake, mirroring the melancholy mood inside the tent. Emily shifted closer to John on the chilly late August night in the Boundary Waters of northern Minnesota.

"How is this our last night together?" John's silky baritone voice whispered into her ear. Even after a whole summer together, his voice still heated her skin and sent goosebumps racing down her neck.

Emily flipped over to face her first true love. Her carefree summer after college graduation had turned upside down when John joined her on staff at Northern Woods. How was she going to survive without him? They'd spent the last nine weeks guiding groups of canoe-campers through the Boundary Waters, surviving harsh elements, grumpy fishermen, and unpredictable weather.

"I can't believe it either."

John was headed to New York City for medical school, while her new job on the flower farm started soon.

"I didn't even know flower farms existed until I met you," said John.

Emily giggled. "Where else would a horticulturist work?" She placed a palm on his chest, his heart beating beneath her hand, strong and steady. "I've got an idea. Let's meet here over the holidays."

"Here?"

"Yeah. We'll stay in the lodge and celebrate together. It'll give me an excuse to escape my drama-filled family." Her parents had sold her childhood home, finalized their ugly divorce, and moved to separate coasts. Her older sister, not wanting to leave their hometown, had shacked up with her loser boyfriend. Emily studied John's face and could practically see the pieces of her plan clicking into place.

"I'll be done with my first semester of med school. My parents travel overseas for the holidays; sometimes I tag along, and sometimes I stay home alone." He hugged her close. "I'd rather be with you this year."

"I'm not sure I can last four months."

John tugged her closer. "Then let's make our last night memorable."

December 1998

Emily cursed her subcompact car's worn tires as she slipped and skidded over the snow-covered gravel drive leading to the Northern Woods lodge. The relentless snowstorm lengthened her drive from the tiny town in southern Minnesota to the Boundary Waters. Could she afford new tires yet? As much as she loved her job working at the flower farm, she didn't have much money left at the end of the month.

When she parked the car, her stomach tightened and sweat beaded on her upper lip. She placed a hand over her still-flat belly. "Okay, kid. Time to break the news."

Her boots sank into the slushy snow of the parking lot, soaking the bottom two inches of her jeans. Dismissing the icy shock and tugging on her knit hat over straight chestnut hair, she turned and faced the lodge.

The large wooden structure, trimmed with white lights, shone against the backdrop of the lofty pine trees of the Superior National Forest. Wreaths with dark-red bows hung from the double wooden doors, and icicles dripped down from the roof, giving the whole structure the look of a gingerbread house. John, dressed in tailored pants and a button-down shirt, waved to her with his arms open wide from the iconic wrap-around porch. Wasn't he freezing?

She scampered up the steps as fast as she could in her heavy winter coat. John wrapped her in his arms, and she buried her face into his shoulder, inhaling his sandalwood scent. He swung her around, and when she pulled back, their chilly lips collided like they'd never been apart.

"C'mon inside," said John. "It's freezing out here."

John led her into the lodge, the place where she worked every summer after college, where she met John, and where they fell in love. The comfy lobby chairs were pushed against the far wall to make room for a nine-foot-tall Christmas tree. The rich aroma of beef wafting from the dining room found its way to Emily's nose, and her mouth watered. The hostess, chef, and lodge director greeted John and Emily with hugs and wild stories from the last four months. When they finally peeled themselves away from the revelry and reached the privacy of their room, the world disappeared.

Darkness crept into the room like an uninvited guest an hour later as they lay satiated in bed after four months apart. John ran a hand along her forehead, brushing a wisp of hair out of her eyes. "Something's different. Is it your hair?"

Her heart thumped in her chest. "It's a little longer maybe."

"I love it."

Relief washed over Emily. She couldn't tell him yet. They'd just reconnected. "Hungry?"

"Starved. Let's go down to dinner."

Emily re-dressed in the jeans and flannel shirt she'd peeled off her body earlier, while John chose a clean outfit of pressed khakis and a button-down shirt from the closet. He fussed with his hair in the bathroom and reapplied a moisturizer to his face while she waited. When he emerged from the bathroom, he clasped a designer watch to his wrist that must have cost more than her last car payment.

"Nice watch."

"Thanks. My parents gave it to me for Christmas before they left for Australia."

"Australia?"

"Yeah. I think they've been everywhere else on the planet. It's a twenty-hour plane ride. No thanks." He hugged her and sighed. "Besides, I'd rather be with you." He kissed her on the forehead before loading his pockets with coins, keys, a linen hanky, and eye drops. After he double-checked his wavy blonde hair in the mirror, he held the door open. "Ready?"

She laughed, and they sauntered down to the dining hall to indulge in the full roast beef dinner worthy of an award if it wasn't on a self-serve buffet. Thankful she could now eat a meal without the threat of nausea, she filled her plate. She passed on the coffee but inhaled the flourless chocolate cake after most of the other guests retreated to their rooms.

Snow fell in big, lazy flakes from the dark sky, illuminated by the exterior lights on the lodge, and Emily shuddered, grateful to be off the roads and safe and warm in the lodge. John rubbed the top of her hand with his butter-smooth finger. "You know, I counted down the days to be with you."

She pulled her gaze away from the window to meet John's cornflower-blue eyes and squeezed his hand. "Me, too. My parents are pissed I'm not celebrating with them, but after the divorce, they made that kind of impossible for me. I don't have the money or time to fly from coast to coast during the holidays. Their divorce cleaved through what was left of our family."

He nodded. "I'm sorry. Families are full of drama. Remember some of the groups from last summer?"

"Boundary Waters trips can be stressful, just like holidays. Stress brings out the crazy in people. That's why meeting here was the perfect plan." She ate a bite of the chocolate cake, the sugary richness coating her tongue, priming her taste buds for a week of treats.

"Remember our last weekend together? We took a trip—just the two of us."

She set down her fork and blushed. "We didn't make it past the first campsite."

Instrumental holiday music piped in from speakers on the rafters, and logs crackled and spit in the fireplace across the room. Emily leaned toward him to close the distance between them. "So, I wanted to tell . . ."

"Sorry, folks." The chef approached their table. "We're closing. Can you move to the lobby?"

"Of course," said John.

On their way out of the dining room, they stopped beside a framed photograph from one of their trips the previous summer. Emily's smile was wide, and John's arm was draped over her shoulder. "It's kinda weird to be guests and not staff," said Emily.

Alone in the dining hall, John placed his lips against hers. The tenderness tingled all the way to her toes. They bypassed the lobby, jumped into an elevator, and hustled back to the privacy of their guest room. Emily melted into John like a marshmallow over an open fire.

Sun splashed the wall the following morning, waking Emily from the best sleep she'd had in months. The silence of snow outside beckoned her from her warm bed to the window, where she opened the blinds and sat in a chair beside it.

"What should we do today?" asked John. "Skate? Ski?"

A pick-up truck plowed the mountains of snow off the lake. She clasped her stomach. What if she fell on the ice? Skating might not be the best idea. "Ski?"

"You got it. After lunch I thought we could go into town and shop and visit the café. Or maybe we could hit up that new brewery down the road. Hmm. I wonder if they're open during the holidays? I've made reservations at a restaurant closer to Duluth for dinner. The lodge food is great, but it's Christmas Eve. I want tonight to be special." He bounded out of bed, kissed her on the cheek, and belted out a jazzy rendition of a Christmas song as he got in the shower.

Emily wrapped a blanket around her shoulders and hugged her knees. Did she have the energy for skiing, shopping, and dinner out? She definitely needed to tell him her news before they went to a brewery. Why was she waiting? He deserved to know about their baby. Maybe she should've told him over the phone months ago. She shook her head. No. She'd wanted to tell him in person. John sang louder in the shower. She bit her lip. Ugh.

A cardinal flew a streak of red across the property and landed in a nearby pine tree while a squirrel tracked across the blank canvas of snow. Movement near the side of the lodge caught her eye. What was that? She squinted out the window, cursing herself for leaving her glasses in the car. A person moved against the wall of the lodge and looked side to side before lifting the dumpster lid and climbing in.

"John," Emily shouted. She shook her head and looked again. "John. C'mere."

John emerged from the bathroom wearing only boxer shorts and a smooth green substance all over his face.

"What the hell is that?" Emily asked.

"Don't judge me. I'm pore challenged. What's the matter?"

"I just saw someone dive into the dumpster."

John tilted his head. "Are you sure? Where're your glasses?"

She ignored his question. "Someone approached the dumpster, looked around, and jumped in. I swear."

"Probably a raccoon or something." John retreated to the bathroom and took up his humming.

Emily strained to see if something emerged from the dumpster, but nothing caught her eye.

Cross-country skiing in the woods behind the lodge kept Emily's feet on the ground and the chance of falling to a minimum. The trail cut through a swath of thick pine trees, and John skied in front of her, his long legs and powerful shoulders plowing through the fresh-fallen snow. Her belly flip-flopped. Why did they have to live so far apart? Then again, it might not matter. If he wasn't thrilled about the baby, she'd be on her own anyway.

A flash of blue zipped between the trees. She slowed on the trail and John turned around.

"You alright?"

"I saw something."

He shook his head and moved forward at a steady pace. Her mind drifted, and she didn't notice John veer off the trail, deeper into the woods. All of a sudden, her skis slid under his before she could stop. "Why'd you stop?"

John put a finger to his lips. "Listen," he whispered.

A woman's voice sang "Silent Night" in perfect pitch. The sweet, clear sound echoed through the trees. Emily scanned the area and pointed to a gray tent nestled among the pines.

"It can't even be fifteen degrees. Someone's camping out here?" John whispered to her.

"Winter camping with a hot tent and wood-burning stove is popular up here, but that's a summer tent. Besides, isn't camping on Christmas Eve strange? Should we check it out?"

John nodded and they clipped off their skis and leaned their poles against a tree. He led the way through the white-dusted pines. The singing stopped as they approached. Emily pulled on John's parka and mouthed, "Let me."

"Hello?" Emily asked. "Are you alright? Can we help you?"

Rustling sounded in the tent, and then a child cooed. "Mommy? Are they here for us?"

"Shh."

Emily bent down in front of the flimsy tent and ran her fingers over a rip covered with tape. The rusted zipper didn't close all the way. "We're staying at the lodge. It's pretty cold. Can we help you?"

The zipper opened an inch, and a woman with dirt-smeared cheeks and cracked lips peered outside. Dark circles rimmed her eyes, and she avoided looking at Emily. "Please don't tell anyone we're here. Please. We're not hurting anyone. Just leave us alone."

"I'm Emily. This is John. How can we help you?"

"I don't need anything. Just leave me alone."

A sweet toddler with hollow cheeks and big brown eyes peeked out of the tent zipper and looked at Emily with a serious expression. "We can't leave because Santa knows we live here, and he's coming tonight."

John squatted to the ground to look the little girl in the eye. "Santa's a really smart guy. He'd find you anywhere."

"It's Christmas Eve," said Emily. "How about you join us in the lodge for a meal? Our treat."

A panicked look flashed across the woman's face. "No, no. We're fine here."

"Can we bring you anything?"

A tear escaped the woman's eyes and dripped down her cheek. "Lila, stay here. I'm going to talk to these nice people. Play with your doll; I'll be right back." The woman climbed out of the tent and stepped away from the structure. Her scuffed tennis shoes sank in the deep snow. Emily could almost feel the icy cold snaking up the woman's calves.

"We're fine. Really. We've only been here for two days. I, um . . . had to leave. I'm on my way to the local shelter, but it's Christmas Eve, and I have a four-year-old who is desperate for Santa to come." The woman swiped a tear from her cheek and pulled a small plastic toy from her pocket. "This is all I have to give her, but she needs the magic one last time because life is about to get really hard."

Emily's stomach twisted when she realized they'd come upon a single mom, alone for the holidays, desperate to give her child the magic of Christmas in the woods. What had driven the woman into the frigid wilderness with a four-year-old? Emily clasped her hands together; her fingers numb inside her gloves. The woman and little girl had to be freezing. "It's cold. Please. Come back to the lodge with us."

The young woman shook her head and bent at the waist, grimacing. When she righted her posture, she blew out a breath.

"Are you alright?" asked John.

"I'm fine; it's just a pulled muscle."

Emily put a hand on the woman's back. "It's Christmas Eve."

The woman jerked her body back from the touch. "Please. Leave us alone and don't tell anyone we're here."

"How about we bring you some food?"

The young woman chewed her bottom lip. "Well . . ."

Adrenaline surged through Emily's veins. Food. It was the least they could do. "We'll be back."

The woman nodded and retreated into her tent.

Emily and John hiked back to their skis.

"Shouldn't we bring them back to the lodge with us? Call the cops?" said John.

"No. She's scared someone will find her. We'll start with food. Maybe after she eats something she'll be more agreeable. I'm guessing they're both starving. Let's ask the desk if there's an available room. We can tell them you're sick or something and need separate rooms. If she agrees to come back with us, we'll have a room ready for them."

"Good idea." John led the way to the trail, and they skied with purpose back to the lodge. While John returned the rented skis, Emily inquired about another room at the desk.

The host tapped her chin with her pen. "Um, sure. Is there a problem with your room?"

"John's not feeling well. He's been keeping me up at night. You know how it is, right? First, he blows his nose, and then the coughing starts. After he uses the bathroom, he comes back to bed and tosses and turns till morning." Emily rolled her eyes for emphasis. "I just need a good night's sleep."

The host raised one eyebrow. "Got it. I've got one room left, but it only has one double bed."

"Perfect." Emily handed over her credit card, prayed she had enough in reserve for another charge, and accepted the key for the new room.

John and Emily went up to the room to double-check it had clean towels. "Do you think she'll come back to the lodge?" asked John. "That tent has to be freezing."

"Food may help sway her, especially if she's the one I saw hopping into the dumpster."

"Let's grab lunch, and then we'll hike back out to the woods with the food. While they're eating, we'll convince them to come back and stay in the room."

"Good plan."

Armed with turkey sandwiches, chips, and cookies from the lunch buffet, Emily and John braved the elements on foot to visit Lila and her mom in the woods. Upon arriving at the tent, they heard the toddler whimpering.

"Lila?" asked Emily.

The zipper opened a crack. Lila's tear-streaked face appeared. "Mommy doesn't feel good."

Emily entered the tent and bent down to the woman. She touched her forehead and turned to John. "She's burning up."

She bent toward the woman. "It's Emily and John. We brought some food, but we need to get you to a hospital."

The woman grabbed her arm. "No. No hospital. He'll find me."

"At least let us take you back to the lodge."

The woman looked toward her daughter. Lila clutched a blankie to her cheek and sucked her thumb, shivering in one corner of the tent. Her vacant, red-rimmed eyes stared at her mommy.

"Okay," the woman whispered.

Emily tied Lila's shoes and helped her out of the tent. John grabbed the small plastic grocery bag filled with clothes and toiletries while the little girl snuggled onto Emily's shoulder with her blankie and doll. John hoisted the woman up and into his arms as if she weighed nothing.

They hiked back to the lodge along the trail. John waited on the side of the building with Lila and her mom while Emily distracted the host with questions about a photograph in the dining hall, and then he hustled Lila and her mom up the back stairs to the guest rooms.

Emily inserted the key and opened the guest room door. John laid the woman on the bed. She moaned and curled up into a ball while Lila whipped off her coat before scampering into the bathroom.

"Do you need help?" asked Emily.

"Nope. I'm a big girl."

Lila asked for help washing her hands. Emily soaped the paper-thin skin of the toddler's hands, dirt pouring down the drain. When was the last time Lila and her mom had access to running water or a bathroom? Emily dried Lila's small, perfect hands with a soft, warm towel, and the little girl smiled at her with a toothy grin.

When they emerged from the bathroom, John waved Lila over to the desk, where he had arranged a portion of the sandwich and chips. She climbed up onto the chair, sinking her teeth into the bread, smiling again. John helped her as she grasped the water glass with both hands, drinking her fill. Color returned to Lila's cheeks as her mom stirred on the bed.

The woman opened her eyes and looked around. "Lila?"

"Right here, Mommy." Lila waved from the desk, her feet swinging beneath the chair. "The sandwich is yummy."

"We're in the lodge," said Emily. "No one saw us bring you and Lila inside. What's your name?"

"Um, Julie."

Emily was pretty sure Julie wasn't her name but didn't question her. "Okay. Julie, you have a fever. Have you been sick?"

She shook her head. "I have a little cut." She lifted her shirt to expose an ugly knife wound across her stomach. Bile surged up Emily's throat, and she looked away.

John bent toward Julie. "I have some medical training. Can I take a look?" He poked and prodded the area. "It's not deep, but it's infected. The wound needs to be cleaned and dressed. You should be on an antibiotic."

"No doctors." Julie patted the bed, and Lila snuggled beside her. "We don't mean to cause trouble. We were fine in the woods," she sighed. "But it's so much warmer here."

Emily pulled John aside. "Why don't you go get some supplies to bandage her wound, and I'll see if I can't get her to wash up and eat?"

"She probably needs an antibiotic. I can't do that for her."

"Just get what you can to clean the wound."

"Okay. I'll be gone for at least an hour."

"Thanks," said Emily. She kissed John, and he left a minute later.

She poured Julie a glass of water and turned a cartoon on the TV for Lila. Julie sat up in bed and sipped the water.

"When was the last time you ate?" asked Emily.

"A couple of days. I've given all the food I've found to Lila."

Emily broke off a piece of the sandwich. "Small bites."

Julie nibbled a bite of the sandwich and crunched a chip. She drank the water and licked her cracked lips.

"How about a shower?"

She shook her head. "I don't want to shower with the cut. I'll wash up in the sink."

Lila lay back on the pillow and fell asleep while her mom used the bathroom. Emily removed the little girl's too-small shoes, ignored the dirty socks, and covered her with the bedspread. Her tiny frame disappeared under the sheets.

Julie returned from the bathroom, hands and face clean, and leaned back against the pillows on the bed. She nibbled at the food. "I'm so sorry to ruin your holiday."

"You didn't ruin anything."

"Your husband seems really great. Do you have kids?"

Emily shook her head. "John's the love of my life." Did she just admit that to a stranger? Some part of her had always believed it but saying it out loud was different. "We're not married, though."

The flutters of life growing inside her belly reminded her again to break the news to John. Would their long-distance relationship be enough? What about after the baby was born? There were so many unanswered questions. Lila started to snore.

John returned an hour later with the medical supplies. He cleaned and dressed Julie's angry, red wound. She joined Lila in sleep minutes later. Emily and John tiptoed out the door and retreated down the hall to their own room.

"Now what?" asked Emily.

"I picked up a pamphlet on local women's shelters when I was in the pharmacy. There's one not far from here."

"That's probably where they were headed."

"They need a couple of days to heal and eat. I'd like to monitor the wound."

"I don't even want to think about who did that to her or why. At least she's alive." Emily spied a bag in the corner. "What's in the bag?"

"I had fun playing Santa."

Emily opened the bag to find an adorable snowsuit and winter boots for Lila, a book of fairy tales, feminine hygiene products for Julie, and warm hats and gloves for both of them.

"I thought we could wrap everything up and have it ready for them when they wake up in the morning."

Emily sniffed. "This. This is why I love you so much." John held her tight as she cried on his shoulder, exhausted from the emotional day.

They skipped their reservation at the fancy restaurant and brought chicken, potatoes, beans, and chocolate chip cookies to Julie and Lila, who both looked better after their naps. Lila begged John to play I Spy, and after the rousing game, she jumped on the bed. "Mommy, we should live here." The little girls' laughter filled the room until her eyes drooped, and her yawns replaced her giggles. Emily and John said goodnight and locked them inside the warm room.

Emily faced John in the hall. "Let's wrap their gifts. You grab some newspaper from the lobby, and I'll sneak outside and borrow one of the ribbons from the wreath on the door. We'll return it tomorrow, but they need a little color to celebrate."

"You're the best. You think of everything. Meet you back in our room."

Once everything was wrapped, they crept into Julie and Lila's room and laid all the packages and the big, red bow on the desk as they slept.

Christmas morning dawned with snow flurries and a sub-zero temperature outside. Emily cozied up in bed with John.

"You're great with Lila," he said.

Her heart fluttered and she inhaled a deep breath. "Um, yeah. So, I've been meaning to—"

His rosy lips parted into a broad smile as he interrupted her. "I might want a couple of kids someday."

Emily's pulse raced.

"If they're all as cute as Lila, of course."

"So, um . . ."

John bounded out of bed. "Let's get breakfast. I wanna see Lila open her gifts."

Emily sank into the pillows. What was her problem? Why couldn't she tell him? Maybe once Julie and Lila were safe at the shelter, she'd drop the news.

They carried plates loaded with eggs, toast, muffins, sausage links, and an assortment of jams up to the room. They knocked and Emily called, "Julie? Lila? Can we come in?"

The door cracked open, and Julie smiled when she saw them. Lila jumped up and down, pointing to the presents on the desk. "Santa came! Santa came!"

"He sure did," said John, swooping Lila into his arms. "Wow. Are you going to open them?"

"Yup. Mommy said we had to wait."

Emily watched their exchange and placed her hand on her belly. Julie gave her a knowing look and accepted the food.

Lila opened all the gifts and tried on her new snowsuit and boots. Sweat poured off the little girl's forehead as she danced around the room in the warm outfit.

"We should really get to the shelter," said Julie after another exciting game of I Spy.

John nodded. "We can take you there."

"No. You've done enough for us already. We can walk. Besides, Lila has a snowsuit now."

Emily placed her arm around Julie's shoulder. "Please. Please let us take you."

A tear escaped Julie's eye. "Alright," she whispered.

"I'll warm up my car and distract the hostess," John said before leaving the room.

Julie looked at Emily as she gathered their belongings. "When are you due?"

"What do you mean?"

"You're pregnant, right?"

Emily blushed. "How did you know?"

Julie shrugged. "You have the look, and you cradle your belly."

Emily sank onto the bed. "I haven't told John. I'm afraid. We live far apart. He's on the East Coast in medical school, and I'm working in southern Minnesota. We really haven't even known each other that long. What if he doesn't want the baby?"

Julie sat beside her and held her hands. "He's great with Lila, and it's obvious he loves you. Tell him."

Emily nodded. "Thanks."

They made their way down the back stairs. "Are you sure there's nothing else we can do for you?"

"You've done more than enough. The shelter is where we need to be. We've been there before. Thank you for the ride, the food, for . . . everything."

John buckled Lila into the backseat of his rental car, and Julie slid in beside her. Emily rode in the front seat and looked out the window as John and Lila belted out Christmas tunes for the whole ten miles.

A woman met their car at the entrance, ushering Julie and Lila through a tall metal gate. The gate slammed shut, and they disappeared into the safety of the shelter.

Emily closed her lips around the last forkful of mashed potatoes and swallowed the buttery goodness in the lodge on Christmas night. "Hey, I'm sorry we didn't make our reservation last night."

"No worries. It was more important to help them. I'm so glad they're safe now. We'll get to the restaurant later in the week." John offered her a decorated sugar cookie in the shape of a snowflake. "Let's skate tomorrow. It'll be great. The lodge rents skates, and the ice on the lake is as smooth as glass."

Emily was about to bite the cookie but shook her head. "No. I don't think so."

"Oh, come on. I know it's cold, but I haven't skated in years. I'll even hold your hand."

"No." Emily tossed the cookie onto her plate and crossed her arms over her chest. "I can't."

"Why not?"

"Because . . ." Her eyes flooded with tears, blurring John's face. "Because . . . I'm pregnant," she whispered.

John's eyes widened, and he leaned toward her. "Pregnant? Are you sure? Is it . . . is it?"

She nodded. "Yes, it's yours. I'm due in May. I wanted to be sure before I said anything, and I wanted to tell you in person."

He sank back into his chair, stunned into silence.

Tears dripped down her cheeks. "I thought I'd be able to do everything myself, but after meeting Julie and Lila . . . I want to be together. I don't know what to do."

A broad smile broke out on John's face then. "This is fantastic!"

Emily swiped her wet cheeks. "What?"

John handed her the soft hanky out of his pocket to dry her face. "I have something to tell you, too." John leaned toward her, their faces almost touching. "I dropped out of medical school two months ago and became an EMT."

"You quit medical school?

"Yeah. I hated it. The classes, the stress, and the city itself grated on me every day. I haven't told my parents yet. They're gonna kill me. But I love being an EMT. I'm already helping people."

"Wow. You didn't like the city?"

John shook his head. "The crowds and noise drove me nuts. The smells. I don't think I'll ever get the subway stench out of my nose completely. My plan was to come here, woo you with excellent cuisine, and ask you about me moving to Minnesota to give our relationship a chance. I knew there was a reason I hated the city." He planted a loud kiss on her lips. "It's because I'm meant to live in Minnesota with you and our baby."

"So, you're moving closer to me?"

"Yup. I love this region of the country, and I love you. Being an EMT has taught me to live every moment of every day. I'm giving up a doctor's salary, so we might not have a super fancy life."

Emily looked around at the old lodge dining hall with canoe paddles hanging over the door, paper napkins on the table, and a self-serve buffet. "The baby and I don't need anything fancy; we just need you."

December 1999

John parked Emily's old subcompact car in the Northern Woods lot, and Emily gazed up at the wooden lodge, blanketed in snow, lights glowing inside. She leaned across the console and kissed John on the cheek. "Thanks for bringing us here. The staff really wants to meet the baby."

They both turned and looked into the backseat where their six-month-old slept in her car seat, her feet reaching the edge, her mouth moving in her sleep.

"Of course. Northern Woods is family and will always be home."

They piled out of the car, Emily carrying the baby while John held her elbow up the slick wooden steps. Ooh's and aah's from the staff greeted them in the lobby. Emily passed the baby to the director and felt a tug on her jeans. When she looked down, Lila beamed up at her. Julie stood beside her daughter wearing an apron and a nametag that read *Anne*.

"Oh! What a surprise." She bent down to hug the little girl, taller and missing a tooth.

"We heard you were coming for the holidays, and I helped Lila remember how you saved us from freezing in the woods last year."

Emily touched Anne's arm. "Are you safe?"

She smiled. "I am. He's gone, and I got a job in the lodge kitchen in the spring. We live on the property in a little cabin. Lila loves it."

"I'm sure she does. It's home."

About the Author

Amy Hepp writes contemporary romance from her screened-in porch amongst the birds and blue skies of Raleigh, North Carolina. Her stories are set in the fiercely protected Boundary Waters wilderness area of northern Minnesota, providing an idyllic backdrop for her characters to fall in and out of love. Amy has published two books (*Northern Woods, Ripple Effects*) through Fifth Avenue Press, Ann Arbor, and contributed short stories to two anthologies (*Craving You, Just One...*) through And You Press/Nicole Frail Books. A short story ("Finding Peace"), forthcoming, won honorable mention in a recent contest by the Wake Forest Review.

You can find Amy on Instagram and Facebook:
@amyheppstories

To learn more about Amy, visit her website at:
https://amyheppstories.wixsite.com/my-site

Contributors' Library

Please also look for these titles, which were written by, published by, or feature the authors in this anthology.

A Beautiful Lily
Caroline Baccene

Breathing in the Fog
Caroline Baccene

The Charred Grape
Caroline Baccene

A Serendipitous Summer
includes "First Time?"
Caroline Baccene

The Catalyst
Nat Bickel

The Christmas Clue
Nat Bickel

The Volcano No One Could See
Nat Bickel

12 Knights of Christmas
includes "Being Mrs. Claus"
Melissa Cate

Welcome Home
Melissa Cate

The Ghosts in Maple Leaf Gardens
Rick Ferguson

All Year With Anthony
Katie Fitzgerald

Coming Back to Christmas
Katie Fitzgerald

Perfect on Paper
Katie Fitzgerald

Northern Woods
Amy Hepp

Ripple Effects
Amy Hepp

Another Fish in the Sea
Amy Kelly

Prairie Tale
Amy Kelly

Belladonna's Garden (Issue 1)
includes "The Taste
of Nettles"
Amy Kelly

*emerge25: The Writer's
Studio Anthology*
includes "Book Snub"
Amy Kelly

Not As It Seems
includes "A Killer Dream"
yesenia monique

Kaleidoscopic Quill
includes "Batesia Hypochlora"
Morgan Matlow

Just One…
includes "Chapped Lips"
Katherine Rea

*The Greatest Holiday Romance
Stories Ever Written*
features "The New Year's
Black-Tie Affair"
Laura Turner

*Midnight, Mischief &
Mistletoe*
features "A New York Kind
of Holiday"
Laura Turner

About the Editor

Nicole Frail has been a professional editor of fiction and nonfiction books for adults and children since 2009. Between 2012 and 2024, she worked as an acquisitions and project editor for a traditional publisher based in New York City while simultaneously working with independent/self-publishing authors via her small business, Nicole Frail Edits.

In mid-2024, Nicole switched gears and decided to take her "side gig" full time, expanding the services offered through Nicole Frail Edits, LLC. Shortly after, she formed her own small press, Nicole Frail Books, LLC, to publish anthologies born out of short story contests as well as ebooks and other projects still to come. NFB now has three imprints: And You Press, Attic Ebooks, and InkBridge Books.

Nicole lives just outside Scranton, Pennsylvania, with her husband, three little boys, and two Tuxedo cats.

You can find Nicole Frail on Instagram, Facebook & Bluesky as:
 @nicolefrailedits & @nicolefrailbooks

And visit her websites at:
 www.nicolefrailedits.com
 www.nicolefrailbooks.com

Acknowledgments

Thank you to the following for all of the support, trust, and excitement they've shown me and my little press throughout this process, especially while juggling multiple anthologies with release days a week apart from each other!

To ALL of the authors who submitted to the short story contest, thank you for finding the prompt enticing enough to want to write about and for sharing your enthusiasm for it!

To the authors featured in *Home for the Holidays*, this is such a special collection of stories, and I am so proud of how deep so many of you dug for your content. I appreciate the ways you've shown up for this book!

To Happily Booked PR for managing our ARC team for this book, thank you!

To Catti-Brie Kunkelman, one of my 2025 student interns, for being an absolute *rock star!*

To Lori Green, my graduate assistant, with her eye for the smallest of details *and* super helpful content-related observations. (I appreciate you!)

To the NFB Street Team, for being adaptable, enthusiastic, supportive, and overall awesome. We're growing, little by little, and I am grateful to you all.

To the local NEPA readers who continually show up at craft fairs and vendor events and are eager to get their hands on these anthologies: you make my day every time you stop by to say hi and see what's new. *heart hands*

And, as always, I'm forever grateful for my reasons for every season: Matthew, Cooper, Travis, and Eli.

Another Chance to Get It Right: A New Year's Eve Anthology
9 Stories

As the Snow Drifts A Cozy Winter Anthology
9 Stories

Craving You A Spicy Valentine's Day Anthology
12 Stories

Recipes for Romance A Sweet Valentine's Day Anthology
19 Stories

Anthologies

Just One . . .
A Summer Romance
Anthology
12 Stories

Not As It Seems
A Gothic
Anthology
17 Stories

The Gift Exchange
A Young Adult Holiday
Anthology
10 Stories

Home for the Holidays
A Christmastime
Anthology
12 Stories

And You Press, or &You Press,
is an imprint of Nicole Frail Books, LLC,
an independent ("indie") publishing
company located in Avoca, Pennsylvania.

And You Press was created to release the anthologies built from the short story contests that launched NFB in the fall of 2024. The name reflects the requirement that every book published under this imprint will have multiple collaborators so that every title released brings multiple voices to each project.

These titles may be additional anthologies, novels with two or more authors, author and illustrator teams, or something else entirely. As long as the work has multiple creators who will be credited equally for the work they've put into it or will put into it, it may be appropriate for this imprint.

To learn more about submitting a query to And You Press, visit www.andyoupress.com.

Readers!

Join the NFB Street Team for exclusive first reads and swag from And You Press!
www.nicolefrailbooks.com/street